NIGHT OWL

UPSIDE★DOWN MAGIC

NIGHT OWL

by

Sarah
MLYNOWSKI,

Emily
JENKINS,

and

Lauren
MYRACLE

SCHOLASTIC PRESS/New York

Library of Congress Cataloging-in-Publication Data available
ISBN 978-1-338-66216-0

1 2021

Printed in the U.S.A. 23
First edition, June 2021

Book design by Abby Dening

With big, magical wishes for the future, this book is dedicated to: Anabelle, Chloe, Hazel, Ivy, Alisha, Mirabelle, Maya, Jamie, and Al.

1

Here is what Elinor Boxwood Horace packed for the Dunwiddle Magic School Fifth-Grade Sleepover on Big Night:

1 water bottle with sparkly stickers on it

1 pair of plaid pajamas

1 sleeping bag, belonging to Aunt Margo

1 favorite pillow

1 second-favorite pillow

1 toothbrush and 1 adorable tiny tube of
   toothpaste, safe in a plastic baggie

1 hair scrunchie

1 pair of purple jeans and a bright blue
    sweatshirt with sequins on it, to wear
    the next day

Plus 1 pair of underwear, of course. And socks.

Nory felt a lot of *feelings* about the Big Night sleepover.

For one, she was EXCITED.

All the fifth graders would sleep overnight at school, staying up late for Big Night, the holiday to celebrate the longest night of the year. They'd eat traditional Big Night treats and make paper owls.

There would be a scavenger hunt. The winning team would get an amazing prize: the key to a *secret room* somewhere on the grounds of the school.

But Nory was also SAD.

Her best friend, Elliott Cohen, wouldn't be at the sleepover. He was going to the Sage Academy Big Night Concert instead. In fact, Elliott was leaving Dunwiddle Magic School to go to boarding school at Sage Academy after the winter break.

Leaving!

Dunwiddle!

Forever!

Because of this terrible plan, Elliott had chosen to go to Sage's concert over Dunwiddle's sleepover.

How could he miss their last night of fun together?

So Nory was excited about Big Night, and at the same time sad, and on top of all that, NERVOUS.

Why? Because some kids at Dunwiddle were mean about upside-down magic. In particular the Sparkies, a group of Flare kids with unpleasant attitudes. If something wonky happened at the sleepover, the Sparkies were sure to be mean about it. Like if Nory's friend Bax turned into a rock. Or if her friend Willa made it rain on their sleeping bags.

Nory's own magic could go wonky, too. She could accidentally turn into a squid-puppy in front of the whole fifth grade!

Here's how magic worked: When you were young, you were just a regular kid. You didn't know what your magic would be . . . yet. You went to ordinary school.

Then, shortly after your tenth birthday, your powers bubbled up. You got one of five talents.

Flares had fire magic.

Flyers could fly.

Fuzzies had a magical connection to animals.

Flickers had invisibility magic.

And Fluxers could turn into animals.

Most beginner Fluxers started off turning into kittens. When they got their kittens right—with straight whiskers, four legs, and nice sharp kitten teeth—they started learning to do puppies. Later, they would learn other mammals, like goats and hamsters. In high school, they fluxed into wilder animals, like apes and deer. Birds, insects, and large carnivores could be learned if you went to college.

Nory was a Fluxer, but she mixed up her animals. Kitten was the only animal shape she could hold for more than a couple minutes, and even doing *that* had taken her tons of practice. When she fluxed, Nory often added dragon to her kitten and became a dritten. Or she added goat to her kitten and became a koat. Or squid to her puppy and became a squippy. Stuff like that.

The bright side: Nory had some pretty big power. At age ten, she had already fluxed into a couple of shapes with bird elements. And a couple of shapes with fish elements. Plus one with a touch of mosquito.

The other bright side: Because of Nory's upside-down magic, she now lived with Aunt Margo and went to a new kind of experimental class, one for kids with unusual magic. Her teacher, Ms. Starr, helped each kid in Dunwiddle's Upside-Down Magic class figure out how to manage their own unique powers.

The UDM kids had become a team. They had one another's backs and did their best to understand each student's unusual magic. They stood up for their friends and had a lot of laughs.

It wouldn't be the same without Elliott.

Aunt Margo and her boyfriend, Figs, were waiting downstairs when Nory lugged her duffel bag into the living room.

"Have fun at the sleepover," said Figs. "And keep an eye out for Big Night owls."

"Silly man," said Aunt Margo. "Big Night owls are invisible."

According to legend, Big Night owls were an invisible breed of owls that visited people on Big Night. Nory would never get the chance to see one, obviously. They were invisible. But she always hoped she might hear the beat of their wings.

"Do you believe they're real?" she asked. "The Big Night owls?"

Figs pretended to be insulted. "Excuse me? Of course they're real!"

Nory rolled her eyes, because yeah, yeah, yeah, he had to say that. And anyway, she was glad he did, because she liked believing in them, too.

"Owls are nocturnal," Figs added. "They're the perfect animal to visit us on Big Night since Big Night is the longest night of the year."

"Also, owls have keen eyesight," Aunt Margo said. "They see things clearly even from far away, and we try to do that, too, when we make our Big Night resolutions."

She pointed at the dining table. It was covered with brightly patterned pieces of paper. "Do you want to fold some owls before you go?"

Nory shook her head. "We're folding them at the sleepover."

Nory had folded owls every year on Big Night. The pretty paper and the shape of the owls people often used nowadays were borrowed from Japanese origami, but the tradition of folding paper owls for Big Night had started with ordinary brown paper and tape. People did them all different ways. Nory liked making them, but she had never given the ritual much thought.

"Ms. Starr said we're going to make Big Night resolutions at the sleepover," Nory added, "but this will be my first time. I've always just tossed my owl into the air."

"Ah," said Aunt Margo. "Well, you were young."

"What's my Big Night resolution supposed to *be*?" Nory asked.

Aunt Margo tapped her chin. "It's kind of like a wish, but it's a wish you can make come true for yourself."

A wish you could make come true for yourself. What a cool idea.

Well, Nory certainly wished Elliott was coming to Big Night. And she wished he wasn't leaving Dunwiddle for Sage Academy.

But he *wasn't* coming. And he *was* leaving.

So she couldn't really make a resolution about Elliott, because she couldn't make her wishes about him come true.

"You'll think of something," said Aunt Margo, noticing Nory's silence. "I have faith in you."

Nory put on her jacket and looked in the mirror. There she was: brown eyes, a red sweater, a plaid coat, brown skin, big hair.

She felt a little thrill. It was a holiday. She was staying up late. At school. With her friends! She would think of a good resolution. She would. And she would make the best of this special evening, even without Elliott.

"Happy Big Night," she told Figs and Aunt Margo. She shouldered her duffel bag and headed out into the misty early evening air.

2

Sebastian Boondoggle was an Upside-Down Flicker. He was tall for his age and pale-skinned, with fierce eyebrows. He liked science class and small rodents like gerbils and hamsters. He *didn't* like foods that were covered with bits of greens or chopped tomato. Or clothes with messages or sparkles on them. Sebastian liked things simple and straightforward.

Why was he in the UDM class? Instead of being able to turn things invisible, like typical Flickers did,

Sebastian *saw* things that were invisible. He saw them whether he wanted to or not.

For example, he saw all the things that typical Flickers had turned invisible. Snotty tissues they were too lazy to toss in the trash. Water fountains they had made disappear so they could splash innocent kids with invisible drops of water. That kind of thing.

He also saw sound waves. When the sounds were pleasant, seeing them was cool. Beautiful music looked beautiful, like glittering golden waves. And everyday soft sound waves, like quiet voices or the rustle of paper—those sounds were okay, too.

But loud sounds were painful. They hurt Sebastian's eyes and gave him headaches. Off-key singing made him shield his eyes. So did yelling and jangly school bells.

He did have ways of coping. He could block sound waves from his peripheral vision by wearing a giant cone around his head, like a dog did after it got stitches. He also had a pair of chunky aviator goggles that limited the sound waves coming his way.

But even the cone and the goggles *together* didn't stop his eyes from hurting in certain situations—and unfortunately, Sebastian's problem was getting worse.

His magic was growing stronger.

That happened to everyone as they got older. They learned more skills, but they also developed more power. His classmate Marigold had gone from shrinking things to being able to big them up. And his friend Andres had gone from flying uncontrollably to being able to harness air currents.

So it was no surprise that Sebastian's magic was growing, too. And yet, the way it was happening seemed unfair. Instead of being able to do new stuff, Sebastian just felt new levels of pain.

His dads were great. They respected his needs. They never wanted his eyes to hurt, and home was usually peaceful and quiet. But school was tough, and getting tougher.

Anyway, Sebastian was ready for the Big Night

sleepover. He was nervous about the noise, but he wanted to hang out with his friends. More important, he wanted to win access to the scavenger hunt prize: the secret room.

Having that room would be a game changer for Sebastian. A secret room would be a *quiet* secret room, a haven from the bells and yells and chatter. If his team won, then maybe, just maybe, Sebastian could survive the rest of the school year.

"Are you packed and ready to go, kiddo?" Dad asked. Dad was six foot five and used his flare talent at his job as a chef. He had red hair and laughed long and loud from his belly. Right now, he was chopping onions for dinner.

"I think so, yeah," Sebastian said.

"Then let's do it," said Baba, Sebastian's other dad. Sebastian called him Baba because it was the Chinese word for *father*, and Baba's parents had been born in China. He was an architect and often used his fluxing magic to become a hummingbird so he could view his designs from the air.

"I think maybe I should bring my head cone after all," Sebastian said as Baba grabbed the car keys. "Tonight is gonna be loud, I think. Like, really loud."

"Sounds smart," said Baba gently. "I'll take your duffel bag. Grab your cone and meet me in the car."

The hum of Baba's car was pleasant. Sebastian closed his eyes and leaned back against the headrest, enjoying this moment of peace.

"Have fun with your friends tonight," Baba said when they pulled up to the school. "And go bananas on the scavenger hunt. Your powers are made for this, kiddo."

"Yes," Sebastian said. "That's the plan."

3

Nory didn't mind that the cold nipped at her cheeks. Or that the sun was going down. What she minded was that she was walking to school alone. She almost always walked with Elliott.

Elliott was an Upside-Down Flare—in his case, a Freezer. He could flare weakly, but he had strong ice magic. The teachers at Sage Academy thought that with the proper training, he could be a full double talent, which was very rare.

Nory did understand why Elliott wanted to go to

Sage. It had a beautiful campus. It had great technology, a huge library, and fancy things like a skunk garden, and afternoon tea with cookies. It was super expensive, and Elliott had gotten a full scholarship.

But she wished he wasn't going. And if he had to go, couldn't he have stayed for one last adventure tonight? They didn't have much time left together.

She could hear her footsteps against the sidewalk. She had never walked alone when it was this dark out. The street felt creepy.

"Boo!"

Ahhhhhhhh! Nory nearly jumped out of her shoes.

She felt herself begin to flux, without meaning to. She did that sometimes.

Pop pop pop!

"Nory, it's just me," said a voice. Standing in front of her was Bax Kapoor, her friend from school. But Nory was too far gone to stop fluxing now.

Pop! She had a kitten body!

Pop! Kitten paws!

P-p-poof! Kitten tail!

And also, dragon claws! Dragon teeth! Dragon wings!

Yep, Nory was a dritten. This was her favorite of the mixed-up animals she fluxed into using her upside-down magic. *Oooooh*, she loved her shimmery, powerful dragon wings. And her dragon fire. *Hiss! Hiss!*

Dritten-Nory's mind was more animal than human right now.

"Ahhh!!" cried Bax, ducking as the fire breath roared toward him.

Hisssss!

"Nory, it's me, Bax!"

Hisssss!

"Stop breathing fire at me!"

Hisssss!

"Nory! Human mind! Now!"

Dritten-Nory heard him. She stopped breathing fire and swooped down to land on a fence post. She knew she should be careful about scaring Bax. When he got startled, he tended to flux. And when Bax fluxed, he couldn't turn back without medicine.

Bax was an Upside-Down Fluxer like Nory, but instead of turning into animals, he turned into objects. Most often a rock, but sometimes a piano or a swivel chair. Once, a rain poncho. Another time, a leash.

In human form, Bax was wiry, with short dark hair and medium-brown skin. He wore an oversized black puffer coat, open over a T-shirt for their favorite band, Everyday Cake. "Flux back," he told Nory, "before you set me on fire and I turn into a hydrant or something."

Dritten-Nory jumped down to the ground and fluxed back into a girl. Then she laughed. "I would love to see you turn into a hydrant."

Bax cracked a smile. "Maybe later," he said. "But let's get moving or we're gonna be late for the sleepover."

On the steps of Dunwiddle Magic School, Nory and Bax found Pepper Phan, Nory's other best friend. "So excited!" yelled Pepper.

"So excited!" yelled Nory.

"Sheesh," said Bax, rolling his eyes. "Tell us all how you're feeling, why don't you?"

Pepper the Fierce was short and wore a blue dress and stripy tights. Her long black hair was in two pigtails. She was an Upside-Down Fuzzy. That meant instead of having a magical connection with animals, she terrified them. That ability was great if you wanted to get rid of a mouse problem, or a case of lice. It was not so great when it came to pets. Pepper's parents had to give away their family dog when Pepper's magic kicked in. That had been hard.

Nory, Bax, and Pepper headed into the lobby. It was packed with kids lugging backpacks and overnight bags. There were shouts of laughter.

Through the crowd, Nory spotted a familiar shock of curly hair. Elliott's hair!

No, it couldn't be. Elliott wasn't coming.

But it was him!

She ran past her fluxing tutor, Coach Vitomin, who was flexing his biceps and talking to a kid about nutrition. Past Nurse Riley, the school nurse, and past Ms. Starr, the Upside-Down Magic teacher. Ms. Starr had her braids in a high bun and held her companion bunny in one arm. Several Fuzzy students were clustered around her, stroking Carrot's long, floppy ears.

"I thought you weren't coming tonight!" Nory cried, flinging an arm around Elliott's shoulder.

Elliott grinned. His sweater was too big, and his jeans had a hole in them. His pale cheeks were pink from the cold outside. "I wanted to surprise you."

He had come to the Big Night celebration after all. He'd wanted to hang out with Nory instead of going to Sage's stuffy winter concert.

Nory's breath caught. Was it possible Elliott had chosen Dunwiddle over Sage completely? If so, then—

He'd stay here forever!

They would walk to school together!

And hang out after class!

And do all the things, together, together, together!

"Does that mean you're not going to Sage Academy after all?" Nory asked hopefully.

Elliott looked confused.

"Because you're skipping the winter concert," Nory explained.

"Nah. I'm skipping because we're supposed to get snow tonight," Elliott said. "My parents didn't want to drive two hours to Sage. So here I am." He started bouncing up and down. "Tonight's going to be so fun!" he said, hyped up. "Are you into the whole Big Night owl thing? 'Cause I'm kind of into it. And I heard we can stay up till midnight."

Even though she was disappointed, Nory started bouncing, too. She couldn't help it. It was Big Night!

At the entrance of the school, Coach Vitomin blew an enormous air horn. *WOOOOOONNNGGG!* "Everyone, bring your things into the gym!" shouted Coach. "Find a spot that'll be yours for the night."

Elliott grabbed Nory's arm and they went in. In

a far corner of the gym, they spotted Marigold and Willa from UDM, already laying out sleeping bags. "Over here!" called Willa.

Willa Ingeborg was thin and pixieish, with light skin and corn-silk hair. Like Elliott, she was an Upside-Down Flare. But while Elliott could flare a tiny bit and make ice, Willa couldn't flare at all. She made rain.

Indoors.

Always indoors.

Willa was best friends with Marigold Ramos, whose magic talent didn't fit any of the five Fs. Marigold shrank things, and she could sometimes make them big again. But not reliably. Marigold wore a bright yellow shirt and black jeans with a thick leather belt. Her dark wavy hair was held back with an antique hair clip.

Marigold's sleeping bag was extra large. "I shrank it when my powers first came in," she explained. "And I couldn't big it up again until recently. Only, I bigged it up too much, I think." Then she grinned. "Oh, well. Now it's extra comfy."

After she rolled out her sleeping bag, Nory looked across the gymnasium. Camped out next to UDM were the Flickers, thank goodness. In general, the Flickers got along well with the UDM kids. Nory heard Clyde and Rainey talking about their stash of invisible candy.

On the other side of the UDM kids camped a group of Fuzzies. All of them had stuffed animals on their pillows, since they weren't allowed to bring animal companions. (Carrot, Ms. Starr's rabbit, was okay because Ms. Starr was a teacher.)

The Flyers were at the far end of the room, and the Flares were in the middle. In the center of the Flare group stood the Sparkies. Lacey Clench, Nory's mortal enemy, was stamping her foot and yelling at her friend Zinnia.

"Happy Big Night!" called Andres Padillo. He was another UDM kid, an Upside-Down Flyer. Andres could fly just fine. In fact, he went a lot higher than most beginner flyers could. But he couldn't come down, not easily. Andres had big brown eyes. Today, he wore his dark hair under a bright green knit cap. Right now he had on his brickpack. It was a backpack full of bricks, and it kept him on the floor.

At home, Andres slept on the ceiling, but tonight, he'd use his sleeping bag. His dad had sewn heavy weights into all four corners.

Andres was excited about the scavenger hunt. "My sister, Carmen, won the secret room when she was in fifth grade. She said it's awesome. Also, she said the things we have to find are tough."

"What kind of things?" Nory asked.

"The items are different every year. Carmen said we'll probably have to use magic. She said the fifth-grade sleepover was the most fun she's ever had on Big Night."

Nory felt a spark of hope about Elliott. If the Big Night sleepover was as great as Carmen said it was AND if the UDM kids won the scavenger hunt and the secret room . . . well, wasn't it possible that Elliott could change his mind about Sage?

He would be all, *Hey, Dunwiddle is where my best*

friends in the whole entire world are. Why on earth did I think I wanted to go to stuffy old Sage Academy with its uniforms and strictness and boring assemblies and living away from home? I don't want to do that at all! And now we have the secret room because Nory is a scavenger hunt genius, so that makes me want to stay here even more. Dunwiddle forever!

Okay, then. Nory's resolution for Big Night was clear now. Keep Elliott at Dunwiddle.

It *was* a wish she could make come true for herself. She just had to win the scavenger hunt, get the secret room for their team, and make sure Elliott had the best time in the world doing it.

Once she did all that?

Elliott would stay.

4

Sebastian walked into the gym wearing his goggles. Then he almost turned around and walked back out again.

There were kids everywhere. Their excited chatter came at Sebastian in brightly colored waves. It was kind of like walking into a room and having an ocean wave splash over you. And then another. And another.

You can handle this, he told himself. *You have to handle this so you can win the secret room.*

And then—*WOOOOOOONNNGGG!* Coach

blew the most enormous air horn Sebastian had ever heard in his life. Sound waves zoomed through the gym. Sebastian cowered.

Oh, wow, it was going to be an intense night.

Moments later, Elliott and Nory stood in front of him. "Moon cookies," said Nory brightly. "I got a whole plate."

Sebastian accepted a cookie as they walked over to the UDM camp. Moon cookies were traditional on Big Night: chocolate crescent-shaped cookies sprinkled with glittering sugar crystals. "Pretty good," Elliott said, taking a bite and talking with his mouth full.

"Pretty good?" Nory said. "They're *delicious*."

Sebastian tried his cookie. Hm. He agreed with Elliott.

"Moon cookies are my favorite Big Night food!" yelled Nory. "Do you love them, Elliott? Or do you *love* them?"

Nory had many good qualities. Being quiet wasn't one of them.

"I have got to get my head cone," Sebastian muttered, tossing what was left of his cookie in the trash so he could rifle through his duffel bag.

"You'll be fine," Elliott said, touching his shoulder and glancing nervously at the Sparkies. "Everyone will settle down when Coach starts talking."

Sebastian knew that his cone made him stand out even more than usual. He often got teased when he wore it. He himself didn't care that much. The problem was, the whole UDM group would get mocked as well. Elliott didn't like to be teased, especially by the Sparkies.

Sebastian left his head cone in his duffel.

WOOOOOONNNGGG! Coach blew his air horn again. Again, terribly bright waves of sound barreled through the room.

"People, people!" Coach called. "Mouths shut and eyes up front."

The fifth graders quieted. Sebastian breathed easier as the sound went down.

"As you know, we're here to celebrate Big Night,"

Coach announced. "But does anyone know *why* Big Night is such a special night?"

"Of course," Sebastian whispered to Elliott. "It's the winter solstice, which happens when the North Pole is tilted away from the sun the farthest it can be."

"It's the longest night of the year," Coach boomed. "Isn't that terrific? Isn't that cool?"

Sebastian frowned. The science *behind* it was terrific and cool, but Coach didn't go into that. Instead, he told them details about the sleepover. He explained rules about cooperation and respect. He reminded everyone about the paper owls they'd be making later and how, when they launched the owls into the night, they would make resolutions for the coming year.

"Listen closely for the wings of the invisible Big Night owls," Coach continued. "Maybe they will hover over you as you make your resolutions."

"Yay, Big Night owls," said Nory, hugging herself. "I hope I hear them."

Did Nory believe in Big Night owls?

No, it wasn't possible. There were no known cases of anyone seeing, hearing, or even smelling them. Kids never learned about them in science class. There would be some record of them actually existing, if the owls were real.

"The highlight of the night is our fifth-grade scavenger hunt," Coach shouted. "And as some of you may know, the prize is a set of keys to a secret room on school grounds. A hideout, you might say. The location of the room will be shown only to the winning team. Last year's winners have already cleared out their things. Their keys will be passed on. Believe me, kids: You want this."

Sebastian's pulse picked up. He *did* want it.

The other kids did, too. They cheered and whooped. They stomped their feet and clapped their hands. Sound waves whizzed by Sebastian's eyes.

"Kids!" Coach cried. "Settle down."

Yes, please, Sebastian thought.

No one did, so Coach fluxed. His face turned red. His head bulged, ballooning outward and sprouting tufted ears. He became an enormous orange tiger with large paws and a powerful jaw.

"Rooooaaaarrr!" Tiger-Coach yelled.

Everyone shrank back, squealing.

Zamboozle, Sebastian thought. Tiger-Coach cut an impressive figure: sleek, muscled, and fearsome. He was far more commanding than Human-Coach, who was also muscled, but bald and kind of goofy.

Tiger-Coach bounded across the platform and planted his massive paws in front of him. "Rooooaaaarrr!"

At last, everyone fell silent.

Tiger-Coach's fur rippled. His limbs rearranged themselves as he fluxed back into his human form.

"*I need your total attention*," he said. He scanned the room of students, his expression stern. "If you interrupt me again, I *will* cancel the scavenger hunt."

Kids hushed one another. Coach nodded his approval. Nurse Riley, Ms. Starr, and the Fuzzy teacher began handing out instructions.

"You will all form teams of four or five," Coach

said. "The first thing you'll do is pick a team name. Then you have two hours to collect the items on the scavenger hunt list. On the back of the list, you'll find the rules. Follow those rules. If you don't, you'll lose points."

"Be on our team," Bax said to Sebastian, tapping his arm. To Willa and Marigold, Bax said, "He's, like, a secret weapon in a scavenger hunt. Remember the Sage Academy hide-and-seek?"

"Excuse me, but no," Nory said. "You're going to be on *my* team, Sebastian. Okay?"

Sebastian puffed up. He didn't care whose team he was on. He was just happy his friends valued his magic so much. He *was* a secret weapon in a scavenger hunt. But Bax had asked first.

He would win the keys to the hideout for sure.

5

Nory clutched the scavenger hunt list in her hands and looked at her team. Elliott and Pepper. Her two besties. And Andres. Andres didn't see invisible stuff like Sebastian, but he would be super helpful looking for things in a scavenger hunt since he could fly.

"The secret room does sound really cool," Elliott said.

"Right?" Nory cried. "And when we win, it will be ours." *And then you, Elliott, will never leave,* she thought. "Let's get started."

"Wait, we need to read the other side of our paper," Pepper pointed out.

"Those are just the rules," Nory said, waving her hand. *"Don't be a jerk to other kids. Stay inside the building."*

"Don't stuff grapes up your nose," said Elliott.

Nory laughed. "Exactly. Let's pick a name. What should we call ourselves?"

"You should call yourself the Wonkos," said Lacey Clench, sneaking up behind them. "That would fit you perfectly."

"Go away, Lacey," Nory snapped.

"The Losers?" Lacey said, tapping her boot on the gym floor and pretending to ponder a deep problem. "The Weirdos? The Tragic Failures?"

Nory turned to Lacey, hands on her hips. "You should call yourselves the Rude People with No Manners."

Lacey's eyes narrowed. "We're obviously the Sparkies," she said. "And we're totally going to beat you. The Sparkies are *on fire.*"

"The Sparkies are burnt out," Elliott deadpanned.

"Why are you even here, Ice Boy?" Lacey asked him. "I thought you were going off to boarding school at Sage Academy, because they felt so sorry for you and your wonky magic."

"Ignore her," Pepper said. "We just have to ignore her and focus."

Nory knew Pepper was right. She turned her back to Lacey and waited for her to walk away. So did Elliott and Andres.

It took ten full seconds of tension and wasted time, but finally Lacey announced, "I have to go win a scavenger hunt now. I don't have time to talk to wonkos. Sorry." She left to find her team.

Nory sighed. "We need a name. Can we call ourselves the Greatest?"

"Let's pick something more original," Andres said.

"Yeah," Pepper said. "What about NAPE? Nory, Andres, Pepper, Elliott?"

Hm. Nory didn't want a name that meant the back of a person's neck.

Elliott had an idea. "What about the Don't Eat Paste Kids?"

"Oooh! What about the Paste-Eaters?" Nory asked. "We'll upside-down it."

Elliott laughed. "That's even better."

"Perfect," Nory exclaimed. "We're the Paste-Eaters."

"Fine by me," Andres said.

Pepper nodded. "Me too."

Nory wrote *Paste-Eaters* on the top of the page.

"Okay, Nory, read us the list," Elliott said.

She cleared her throat and read:

SCAVENGER HUNT LIST

1. A roll
2. Blue crayon that is also a red crayon
3. Coruscation
4. High heels
5. Coach's stamp
6. Ghost

7. An object that weighs more than 4 lbs. on the moon
8. An invisible autograph
9. Something forty years old
10. A member of a royal family

The team went all aflutter.

"Coruscation. What is that?"

"No idea."

"And high heels? Wait, don't Lacey's boots have high heels?"

"Oh, no. Lacey isn't going to win, is she?"

"No way. We won't let her."

"Number six is a *ghost*? How are we going to find a ghost?"

"And what about an invisible autograph?"

"Maybe Sebastian will help us."

"But he isn't on our team."

And so on.

It was a tough list. The items were going to be super hard to find, but Nory prided herself on always looking on the bright side of any problem. "Paste-Eaters for the win!" she cheered. "Our upside-down magic will help us do things that no one else can. You know it's true. So let's rock . . . and roll. Get it? Roll? That's item number one."

"We got it," Elliott said. "Let's roll like trolls."

Nory laughed. "We roll like a troll who is on patrol," she said.

"On patrol till we hit a pothole," said Elliott.

"You two are ridiculous," moaned Andres, but he moaned it nicely.

"That's the point," said Nory. "That's why Elliott is essential to my happiness."

"'Cause I'm a patrol troll," said Elliott, very seriously. "She needs me."

Nory really did.

She clapped. "All right, team. Let the good times roll!"

6

Sebastian, Willa, Bax, and Marigold named their team the Awesome Foursome. By the time they finished going over the rules and were ready to set off in search of a roll, the gym was nearly empty.

"Oh, no!" cried Willa. "Everyone's started already."

Sebastian adjusted his goggles, unfazed. He knew that slow and steady often won the race. Besides, he'd seen Nory's team run off without any clear idea of what they were looking for. "Paste-Eaters for the win!" they'd shouted as they sprinted out of the gym.

The name Paste-Eaters came from the UDM kids' favorite song, "Don't Eat Paste," by Everyday Cake.

> *Don't eat paste*
> *But do eat butter*
> *Don't borrow money*
> *But call your mother*

Nory and her teammates seemed to miss the point of the song, though. It was about NOT eating paste. So why would you call yourselves the Paste-Eaters? A simple name like the Awesome Foursome was definitely better.

"Hey," said Bax as they headed into the hall. "Let's go to the cafeteria."

"How come?" asked Marigold.

"Bread rolls," said Bax. "They have hamburger buns in there. You can see the packages while you wait in line for your food."

"Does a hamburger bun count as a roll?" asked Sebastian. "I think it's a bun."

"A bun is a type of roll," said Bax.

"I don't think so," said Sebastian.

"I think it is," Willa chimed in.

"But if you order a sandwich at a deli, you would say whether you want it on a *roll* or a *bun*," said Sebastian. "That shows they're not the same thing."

"When would I be ordering at a deli?" asked Willa. "There's not even a deli in Dunwiddle."

Lacey's team burst out of the double doors of the cafeteria. Rune held a hamburger bun aloft. "Don't bother," he yelled at the Awesome Foursome. "We got the last roll!"

"It's a bun," Sebastian said calmly. "I don't think it will count."

"Maybe you can't tell it's a roll because you've got those thick goggles on," Lacey snarked. "Or maybe you're just *not that bright*? Ah, that must be it. See ya!"

She and the rest of the Sparkies ran off down the hall.

Sebastian didn't care what Lacey said. Nothing nice ever came out of her mouth, so the mean things she said didn't matter. He figured she was probably sad and angry about stuff, inside. Anyway, the Awesome Foursome would be better off with a real roll. "What other kinds of rolls can we find at school?" he asked.

"A roll of quarters?" suggested Bax.

"A sushi roll?" wondered Willa.

But neither of those would likely be at school.

"I know!" cried Marigold. "A toilet paper roll!"

Oh, that was good.

"Let's do it," said Bax. "I'll go get one."

Sebastian grabbed his arm. "No, wait. We have to stay together. It says so in the rules. If we split up to find things faster, we'll have points deducted."

"Fine," Bax said.

"There's an all-gender bathroom by the principal's office," Marigold remembered. "Let's go."

The all-gender bathroom was a single room with a toilet, a sink, and a paper towel dispenser. The Awesome Foursome had to squeeze in tight in order for them all to fit.

"We have a problem," Bax said as soon as they were all inside. "The toilet paper rolls are locked in the dispenser."

"So we open it," Sebastian said.

"But how?" asked Bax. It was one of those dispensers with thick gray plastic around it.

Willa knelt down. "I think I can pry the first roll out."

"I know how these work," said Marigold. "We have to open the plastic top."

"There's a lot of graffiti in here," said Sebastian, glancing at the walls.

"I don't see any," said Marigold.

Sebastian remembered that she wasn't seeing the same thing he was. The graffiti was invisible. "Well, believe me, it's there," he said. "Instead of scrubbing the walls clean, Principal Gonzalez must have flicked away all the ink."

"What does it say?" asked Bax.

"'Gonzalez is mean,'" Sebastian read aloud. "'Anarchy! Anarchy!'"

Bax laughed. "What else?"

"'Clyde is a cutie.'"

Bax laughed again. "For real?"

"Uh-huh." Sebastian continued reading phrases. "'What the zum-zum?' 'Everyday Cake forever.' 'Don't eat the pizza bagels.'"

"Ha," chuckled Bax. "I love the pizza bagels. What else?"

Sebastian moved on to the next wall. "'Marigold is a wonko,'" he read. "Hmm. I bet Lacey wrote that."

"Sebastian!" Willa barked. She stood up. She had gotten the dispenser open and was holding the toilet paper roll in her hand.

"What?"

"What you just said, that Marigold is a—" She broke off. "Why would you tell us that?"

"I'm reading the graffiti. Bax asked what else, so I told him," Sebastian explained.

"It's okay," Marigold said. "It's no secret some people don't like me."

"Yes, well, Sebastian could have kept it to himself," Willa said.

"It's okay." Marigold touched her hearing aid, as if to protect it.

Willa rolled her eyes. "It's not. It was rude."

Sebastian was baffled. "Marigold doesn't care," he reminded Willa. "She said so."

"Yeah," Willa told him. "Because Marigold is used to people saying mean stuff about her, so she tries not to let it bother her. That doesn't mean you should repeat the insults."

Sebastian blinked. "I just read what was there. *I* wasn't insulting her."

Willa frowned. "In the future, think before you read." She took a breath. "And now I would be glad if we could change the conversation before I rain on all of us. You know I rain when I get upset."

They did know.

Bax yanked open the door, and the Awesome Foursome exploded back into the hallway as a small, five-second rainstorm pelted the all-gender restroom.

7

ory's team had solved *roll* by raiding their classroom's game closet. They found a pair of eight-sided dice in the Murderous Reptiles board game. When it was time to present all their items to Coach, Nory would say, "Roll the dice, Elliott!" and Elliott would. Done.

They got *blue crayon that is also a red crayon* with Elliott's flaring powers. He wasn't a strong Flare, but he was able to mush half a blue crayon to half a red crayon by melting the wax in the middle. Also done.

The third item on the list was *coruscation*. That

one stumped them, but only for a minute. Pepper looked *coruscation* up in the dictionary. It meant *something that sparkles*. "I know!" she cried. "Glitter!"

They dashed to the art room, and Andres put a small jar of red glitter into the front pocket of his jeans. Three times done.

Nory felt electric. There were just seven more items between her and the win that might very well keep Elliott at Dunwiddle.

"Number four is *high heels*," Andres read, holding the scavenger hunt list.

"Remember, Lacey already has this one," Elliott said.

"So annoying," said Pepper.

"Are any of you secretly wearing high heels?" asked Nory hopefully.

No, they weren't.

"Well, do any of you have a pair in your locker?"

No, they didn't.

Nory breathed faster. Winning mattered more to her team than to anyone else. They needed an idea, and they needed one fast.

Ooh. Maybe she should jump ahead and do number five. That would speed things up!

She peered at the list. "After *high heels* is *Coach's stamp*. I can do that. He's my tutor."

Elliott nodded.

"Great," Nory said. "Back in a flash!"

A team of Flyers hovered in front of Coach's office door when Nory arrived. Their names were Princess, Wolfgang, Delicata, and Burt.

"He's not here," Princess told Nory. She looked sulky. "We can't get his stamp."

"Nory's the competition," scolded Burt. "You don't need to tell her."

"Do you think he's hiding?" wondered Princess. "Where would a gym teacher hide?"

"Maybe there are postage stamps at the welcome desk?" proposed Wolfgang.

Nory just smiled. She could see into Coach's office, and she knew something they didn't. "Maybe," she said. "Bye, and good luck!"

As soon as the Flyers were out of sight, Nory rushed inside, grabbed a chair, and pulled it up next to a tall filing cabinet. "Hi, Coach," she said to the striped house cat curled on top.

Cat-Coach swished his tail. "Mwwrrp?"

"Ha-ha, it's obviously you. I can't believe those Flyers didn't figure it out."

"Prrwwrrp," said Cat-Coach.

"Okay. What stamp are you supposed to give me?" Nory said, looking around. She spotted a pad of ink on the desk. "Ah. Got it."

She opened the ink pad and held it out. Cat-Coach pressed his paw first in the ink and then on the back of Nory's hand. A perfect paw-print stamp, straight from Coach himself.

"Thanks," Nory said as she hopped down and returned the chair to where she'd found it. "This will really help with my Elliott resolution."

Cat-Coach tilted his head to the side.

"I have this plan to win the scavenger hunt and get him to stay. It's a long story." Nory hesitated. "But

I just might put this pad of ink in a drawer so it's harder to find. That's still fair play, isn't it?"

Cat-Coach swished his tail.

"Oh, come on," said Nory. "A drawer is a totally normal place to look for a stamp pad."

Cat-Coach hissed.

"Seriously? It's just a little friendly competition."

Cat-Coach shook his head.

"Okay, *fine*," said Nory.

Just after she put the ink pad back where she'd found it, Sebastian, Bax, Willa, and Marigold dashed into Coach's office.

"Have you seen Coach?" Marigold asked. "We're on number five and we need his stamp."

Nory paused. Should she help them?

They were her friends . . . but no! She couldn't help *anybody*. The stakes were too high. She clasped her hands behind her back so they couldn't see the stamp on her hand.

"What are you hiding?" Marigold said.

Nory shoved her hands in her pockets. "Nothing."

"You look all gloaty," said Willa.

Nory lowered her voice. "Normally I would tell you. But *my* team needs to win, because if we do, Elliott might stay here at Dunwiddle instead of going to Sage."

"He said that? That he'll stay if your team wins?" Willa asked, eyes lighting up. She and Elliott were good friends.

Nory shook her head. "Well, not in those words. But how could he possibly leave if he had a secret room? There are no secret rooms at Sage."

"There might be," Bax said. "That place has a lot of rooms."

"No!" Nory cried. "There aren't. Trust me. I know Sage. Boring rooms, yes. Stuffy rooms, yes. But secret rooms? No."

"So you think the secret room will be too hard to walk away from?" Marigold asked.

"I hope it will," Willa said. "I don't want Elliott to go."

"Me neither," said Nory. "See, here's my theory. I think Elliott decided to go to Sage because he was wowed by the fancy buildings and the scholarship money. But I don't think he considered everything he'll be losing. Like, how our UDM class is different from anything they do at Sage."

"That's true," said Willa. "He won't have tutoring in the swimming pool at Sage, or learn the UDM magic techniques or anything."

"And worse, he won't have *us*," Nory said. She was so glad Willa understood. "Winning a secret room will remind him how special Dunwiddle is. What good friends we all are. And then, I think, he'll decide to stay."

"It doesn't seem very likely," said Sebastian, furrowing his brow.

"Why not?" Nory demanded.

"Well, he's getting a full scholarship at one of the fanciest schools in the country," Sebastian said. "They have all the tools and support to help him be a double talent. A secret room can't compete with that."

Nory stamped her foot. "It might. Because it's not just a room, Sebastian. It's friendship. It's UDM."

"But is all that more important than a double-talent education?" Sebastian said. "I'm just saying, you should be realistic. We'll all miss Elliott, but he isn't going to stay."

"Sebastian! You're talking about Nory's best friend," Willa said. "And my second-best friend, pretty much. We want him here."

"Could we maybe discuss this later?" Bax said. "Our team wants to win, too, and we don't need Nory to tell us how to find Coach's stamp. Coach is *right there*." He pointed to Cat-Coach, who was curled on the top of the filing cabinet.

"Ohhh. He's fluxed!" cried Willa.

"Zwingo, Bax, you did it!" said Marigold.

Nory left the Awesome Foursome and went to catch up with the Paste-Eaters, running fast to try to forget Sebastian's words.

Dunwiddle's UDM class was the right place for Elliott. She just knew it was.

Her team was still in Ms. Starr's room. "*Coach's stamp*, done," she boasted, showing them her hand. She didn't mention seeing the other UDM team. She didn't want to talk about what Sebastian had said.

"What was the stamp?" asked Elliott, coming over to look. "Ooh, paw print. He fluxed into a cat?"

"Mm-hmm."

Elliott held his hand up for a high five, and Nory slapped it. "So, what did you guys figure out for *high heels*?" she asked.

"Nothing," Pepper moped.

"Seriously?"

"Hey, we asked every single person who came down the hall," said Andres.

Elliott shrugged. "No one wears them. Not even teachers."

"Oh, no," Nory moaned. "We need to think. High heels. High heels. High heels."

Elliott raked his fingers through his hair. "What other kinds of heels are there?"

"Did you think about heels of bread?" asked a voice from the bottom drawer of the desk.

"Carrot," Pepper cried. "We didn't know you were here."

Carrot climbed from the drawer onto the desk-top. She knew how to talk, thanks to Ms. Starr's Upside-Down Fuzzy magic. It gave animals the power to speak human language. Carrot also had an unusual ability to resist Pepper's fiercing magic. It simply didn't bother her.

She was holding a piece of broccoli and nibbled it delicately, speaking between bites.

"High heels seem so uncomfortable," Carrot said. She wiggled her nose. "Don't you think bread would be better? The hard piece at the end is called a heel."

"That won't work," Elliott said.

"Yes," Nory said, feeling hopeful. "Brilliant. Thank you, Carrot. We can throw them up in the air!"

Elliott held up his palm. "We know for a fact that all the bread is gone," he explained. "We ran into Clyde and Rainey and their Flicker team. They took the heels from the last loaf and taped them on yard-sticks, like flags."

"Oh, no. What now?" cried Nory.

"Rabbits talk about heels of lettuce," said Carrot helpfully. "But I don't think humans use the word that way. And anyway, I don't have any lettuce in my drawer. It gets wilty, and then I don't want to eat it. I only like it crisp."

"Lettuce isn't helpful!" Nory said, feeling panicky. "Does anyone have any other ideas?"

Andres shrugged off his brickpack. He dropped it onto the floor and flew up to Ms. Starr's ceiling, away from the others.

"Andres," Nory cried, looking up at him. "Going up to the ceiling when we're having a discussion is not good team spirit!"

"Ugh," said Andres.

"In fact, it's bad team spirit," cried Nory. "Why are you having bad team spirit in a moment of crisis?"

"You're being so anxious," said Andres, rolling as he floated. "It's our last night with Elliott at school.

And this is supposed to be a *game*, remember? Kinda silly? Can't we just have fun?"

No! Nory wanted to yell. *We cannot "just have fun"!*

But of course she wanted Elliott to have fun. So much fun that he wouldn't leave.

Ahh! Fun!

No fun!

Winning!

High heels!

She felt sweaty, and her skin pricked.

"Nory." Elliott was next to her, his hand on her shoulder. "It's okay. We're doing great. Try to breathe, okay?"

"Huh?" Nory said.

"I'm worried about you fluxing."

Oh. Yeah.

He had a point.

Nory did tend to flux when she was worked up. She had already accidentally turned into a dritten once today.

"If you flux," said Elliott, "and you lose control of your human mind, we'll waste a lot of time."

Nory didn't want to lose time. They were short on time already.

"Do you want to hula-hoop with me?" asked Elliott. "Just for a minute?" It was an exercise Ms. Starr used to help them center themselves and get in better control of their bodies and their magic.

"I want to find high heels," Nory told them. "As fast as possible."

"This will only take a second," said Elliott. "Just a little shortie hoop session. You need a break."

Sigh. "Okay," she said. Nory strode to the Hula-Hoop bin and yanked one out. She brought it to the middle of the rug and started hooping. Elliott and Pepper did the same.

And while she was hooping, Nory didn't think about anything. Not the scavenger hunt, not Sage Academy, not missing her best friend when (if!) he went to boarding school. She couldn't think, because it took so much concentration to keep her hoop in the air.

"Oh," said Pepper suddenly. She let her hoop drop and pointed at Andres. "Look!"

"What?" asked Elliott, still hooping.

"His shoes. The heels of his shoes. They're high."

Nory grabbed her hoop to stop it. "Ha! Yes! Right!" Nory said. "Andres is high, so his heels are high! High heels!"

"Brilliant!" cried Elliott, his hoop clattering to the floor. "People, we really might win this!"

8

As Nory's team ran out of Ms. Starr's classroom, the Awesome Foursome went in.

Sebastian's eyes hurt. He shut the door behind them and sat in his usual seat. Then he pulled off his goggles and closed his eyes.

Ahh. It felt good to see nothing. He put his forearm over his face to block out even more light.

His headache still thumped, but the pain in his eyeballs began to calm. He could function, he thought, if only the sharp pain would go back to a regular, low-level ache.

"Sebastian." Willa's voice was in his ear.

"What?" He kept his eyes closed.

"Are you *napping*?" she asked. "Seriously?"

"I'm just resting," he said. He knew Willa was still mad at him for reading the graffiti. He didn't want to make her angrier by closing his eyes, but he was just *so* uncomfortable.

"Please stop," said Marigold. "We've been talking about the next clue and we need your help."

Reluctantly, Sebastian opened his eyes. He fumbled for his goggles and put them on.

His teammates were pacing with nervous energy. Carrot perched on Ms. Starr's desk, observing them with curiosity.

"Here's where we stand," said Marigold. "We solved *a blue crayon that is also a red crayon* with a purple crayon. Yay, us! And, Sebastian, thanks for knowing what *coruscation* means—Willa's glittery nail polish will count for that. We have our roll of toilet paper and Ms. Starr's high heels. And Coach's stamp, thanks to Bax. But now we need *a ghost*. The rest of us talked about it while you were napping, and—"

"I wasn't napping," said Sebastian. "I can be a better teammate if I rest my eyes."

"Well, it was very, very similar to napping," Willa said. "Right when we're in the middle of a contest."

"Okay," said Sebastian, defeated.

"Can *you* find us a ghost?" Willa asked Sebastian. "By using your magic? That's the idea we had."

"Like, are there any in here with us, right now?" asked Marigold.

"No," said Sebastian.

"Somewhere else at school?"

"No.

"You could try, though," Willa pressed. "Like, look in shadowy corners and shadowy . . . other places. Like closets or something?"

"Ghosts aren't real," Sebastian explained. "So I can't."

"I think ghosts are real," Marigold argued. "And the teachers do, too, or they wouldn't have put *ghost* on the list."

"If ghosts existed, I probably would have seen one," Sebastian explained. "I see invisible people, and a ghost is basically the same thing. But I've never seen anything ghostly, ever. Because there has never been anything ghostly to see."

"Couldn't you try harder, tonight, for our team?" asked Willa.

His shoulders stiffened. "My magic doesn't work that way. I would think you'd know that after being in class with me for so long."

Willa sighed. "Oh, fine. I guess I know. Kind of."

Sebastian felt she should *totally* know. Not *kind of*. He knew how *her* magic worked. Same for *all* the kids in the UDM class. It was important stuff to understand, when all the magics were so wild and different.

"I think our chances of finding a real ghost wandering around the school are about the same as us finding a Big Night owl wandering around the school," Bax said. "Zero."

"Ooooh," said Marigold. "I would *love* to find a Big Night owl."

"Me too. Can you see *them*, Sebastian?" Willa asked.

"No," Sebastian said.

"But this is your first Big Night since your magic came in, so you might," Marigold said.

"They're just not real, either," he snapped. "So I won't."

No one spoke for a moment.

"I wonder if telling a ghost story would count," Bax eventually said. "I know a good one. It's about this ghost with no arms."

Sebastian was grateful for the change in subject.

"No way that will work," interrupted Willa.

"I think it could," said Bax. "The ghost wears a turtleneck but it has no head, and no arms to fill out the sleeves, and it haunts the person who—"

"Let's try something else," said Willa firmly. "We need an actual object, I'm pretty sure."

"I know a ghost," said Carrot, waving at them from her favorite spot on Ms. Starr's desk.

"You do?" asked Willa, going over to her. Willa

and Carrot had a special friendship. Willa often brought the bunny fruit in her lunch.

"Why, yes," Carrot said. "I have a friend named Ghost. She's a mouse. She lives in the air vents. Ghost, can you introduce yourself, please?"

Ten seconds later, a small white mouse crawled out of the air vent under the window. She sat on her hind legs and waved. "Pleased to meet you." Her voice was soft and made only the most delicate of sound waves.

"Ooh, did Ms. Starr magic you, too?" asked Marigold.

"Just last week," explained Carrot. "Now Ghost comes to the classroom and visits, but not when Pepper's here."

Sebastian bent so his face was near the mouse. "Hello, I'm Sebastian. Would you be willing to be part of our scavenger hunt?" he asked politely. "All you'd need to do would be to tell Coach your name."

"Hm," said Ghost.

"And maybe we could, like, do something to thank you for your help?" added Sebastian.

Bax snapped his fingers. "I have string cheese in my desk," he said. "Do you like string cheese, Ghost?" He ran over and pulled out a wrapped piece.

"I do," said Ghost. "I absolutely do."

"You can ride in my front hoodie pocket," offered Sebastian. "I'll keep you safe." He liked the idea of taking care of the tiny, soft-spoken mouse and protecting her from the students' stomping feet.

The mouse climbed onto Sebastian's palm, her claws tickling his skin. Sebastian helped her into the pocket and unwrapped Bax's string cheese. "Here you go, Ghost," he whispered, gently offering the cheese. "You'll be safe with me."

"Thank you," peeped Ghost.

"That was good of you to donate your cheese," Carrot said to the team. "Sometimes animal aid is taken for granted."

"I think Carrot wants something, too," Marigold whispered. "To thank her for the help."

"Right," said Willa. She turned to Carrot and

asked, "Can I bring you some cantaloupe on Monday? To show our appreciation."

Carrot gazed into the distance. "Monday is very far away."

The kids looked in their desks, but none of them had anything a bunny might want. Not even a cough lozenge.

Sebastian had an idea. "I know," he said. "We'll name our team after you. We used to be the Awesome Foursome, but now we will be Friends of Carrot. They'll put your name up on the board and everyone will know how great you are. Will that work?"

Carrot hopped around the top of the desk, contemplating. "Friends of Carrot," she said. "That has a special ring to it. Yes, that will do nicely."

The kids said goodbye and left Carrot hopping around happily, repeating to herself, "Friends of Carrot. What a perfect name for a team."

9

Nory felt bouncy now that they had the high heels solved.

For the rest of the night, she would ignore the flurries and worries in her head and stay upbeat. "Thanks for making me hula-hoop," she told Elliott.

"Here," he said, pulling a squashed moon cookie out of his pocket. It was wrapped in a napkin. "I snagged some snacks to keep up our strength." He broke it in half and gave Nory the bigger piece.

"Awesome," said Nory, shoving it in her mouth.

"And now we're sugar-fueled," said Elliott. "Let's win this thing."

"People, catch up!" Andres called from the hallway ceiling. "We're on *ghost* now. My sister told me the library is haunted, so that's where we're going."

"Haunted?" Pepper asked.

"Supposedly ghosts hang out in the back stacks in the library, where it's creepy," Andres said.

"You don't mean *real* ghosts?" asked Pepper, hanging back a little.

"Real ghosts," said Andres. "Ms. Starr said there used to be mermaids, even though there aren't now, remember? So real ghosts are a serious possibility. Besides, Carmen told me how the lights are always flickering on and off in there. And sometimes there are rattling noises."

"That could be anything," said Pepper. "And anyway, I haven't heard rattling noises. Well, not very often."

They pushed through the library doors and headed for the supposedly haunted stacks. "Hello, ghosts. Are you here?" Elliott whisper-called.

Nory felt a delightful shiver. She put her hand on Pepper's arm. "They're probably friendly ghosts."

"Ooh, like ghosts of teachers who miss being at school," Elliott said.

"Exactly," said Nory. "Or ghosts of librarians who never want to leave the books."

"I don't want to meet any of those people," Pepper said.

Nory held her breath. She listened for rattling sounds.

Nothing.

Would any ghosts actually show up?

They waited.

And waited.

Still nothing.

"Did you guys ever visit the Sage Academy library?" Elliott asked after a bit.

Andres said he'd only seen it from the outside. Nory didn't say anything. She had seen that library a million times, but whatever. She didn't want to talk about it.

"I did," said Pepper. "It was so fancy. I found a deluxe supply closet to hide in. I did my homework there."

"They had so many books. Thousands and thousands. Some of them were rare and super old, but I saw one of the librarians putting stickers on all the new ones. There were, like, stacks and stacks of brand-new books, just piled up like it was nothing."

"Wow," said Andres. "I don't think we get that many new books here."

"I *know* we don't," said Elliott. "I asked Mr. Wang for the new Alex Gino book, and he said he'd spent his budget for this year and couldn't order it."

Ugh. Nory hated hearing Elliott sing the praises of Sage Academy when they were here in this cozy, carpeted, maybe ghost-filled library, the same library where they'd done their Bing Day projects and—well, okay. They didn't actually hang out in the library that much. But the point was, it was the Dunwiddle library! Where Elliott's friends were! And that made it the best.

Anyway, enough talking about Sage. "Ghosts, show yourselves!" Nory called.

The pipes above them rattled.

"Did you hear that?" Andres asked, his eyes lighting up.

"Oh, ghost, hello!" Nory said. "Please help us with our scavenger hunt."

"Or don't," Pepper said. "Ghosts, why are you rattling?" She backed up nervously and bumped into a spinning wire shelf of paperbacks, sending them crashing to the ground. *Bam!*

Nory ran over to her friend. "You okay?"

Pepper clutched a bookshelf and breathed deeply. "Yes," she said. "It was just a rack falling. Nothing else. No ghosts."

Nory set the rack back up. Elliott bent over to pick up some books.

"It's the R.L. Stine rack," Elliott said. "Look how old they are."

"I've read all of them," said Andres from the ceiling.

Nory looked meaningfully at Elliott. "These books

are old. The spines are all cracked, and you know why? Because they've been read by kids going back years and years. It's great to get new books, but these books are *loved*."

Elliott picked up a couple, looking at them. "Yeah, totally," he said. "But the new books at Sage will be just as loved over time. And did you know the kids there are allowed to take out up to forty books on a student ID card? Here, we can only take out two."

Nory sighed. Elliott was Sage obsessed.

"Look at this," Pepper cried, picking up a book by her feet. It was called *The Ghost Next Door.* "It's a ghost. This book will count, right?"

"Definitely," cried Andres. "The rattling led us right to it." He flew toward the door, but stopped and looked at the pipes. "Thank you, ghosts, for rattling us in the right direction!"

An object that weighs more than four pounds on the moon. That was the next clue for Sebastian's team.

"Ugh," complained Marigold as they headed into the hall. "The teachers are trying to make us use science."

"How are we supposed to know how much things weigh on the moon?" asked Bax.

"Do they even weigh anything?" asked Willa.

Bax burped, loudly, as if to say, *Who knows?*

The sound wave was an intense flash of lime green. Sebastian grimaced.

Bax rolled his eyes. "Sheesh," he said. "It's just a burp."

"The sound hurt my eyes," Sebastian said.

"My burp hurt your eyes," Bax stated, disbelieving. "My *burp*."

Yes, it did, Sebastian wanted to say. His headache was getting much worse. But the thought of winning that peaceful, burp-free secret room was keeping him going. He knew the answer, so he explained: "Something on the moon weighs about one-sixth of what it weighs on Earth. We learned this in science class last week. You don't remember?"

Bax raised his eyebrows.

Marigold rolled her fingers in the air. "*Go on*."

"So if something weighs four pounds on the moon, then it weighs six times that much on Earth. Twenty-four pounds." Sebastian massaged his temples. "So we need to find something that weighs more than twenty-four pounds."

"Okay, great," said Willa. "Any ideas?"

"A desk," said Sebastian, pointing back toward their classroom.

"Kid desks aren't that heavy," said Marigold. "We'd have to take Ms. Starr's."

"I don't think Ms. Starr's desk would fit through the door," Sebastian said. "Even if we turn it on its side."

"It had to get in here somehow," Willa said.

Sebastian shook his head. "Not if they put it together inside the classroom."

"We'll take it apart, then," said Willa.

Sebastian sniffed. Were they going to dismantle a desk and put it together again outside in the hall?

Willa pointed at Bax. "You! You can just flux into something heavy."

Bax's eyes widened. "Uh. No, thank you."

"Why not?" Willa asked. "It would solve everything."

"It's not a terrible idea," Sebastian said. "We wait till we've collected everything else. Then, when we get to the gym, Bax will flux into a rock. We won't have to carry anything heavy with us, which is a plus. And we will bring you straight to Nurse Riley's office after we've won."

"Yeah, but I'll miss the scoring and snacks and stuff," complained Bax.

"Come on," said Willa. "You'll barely miss anything. Plus, we'll save tons of time now, because we won't have to search for something heavy. Please?"

"Well . . ." Bax hesitated.

"Pretty please?" Marigold begged.

Bax turned to Sebastian. "You think this is a good idea?"

Sebastian nodded. "I think you'd be doing an important job for the team."

Bax fiddled with his hands. "If I flux, you have to promise not to lose me," he said.

"How could we lose a rock?" Willa asked.

"I mean, don't leave me with *anyone* who isn't a teacher or a kid in our UDM class," added Bax.

"Of course not," Marigold said.

"And remember: I can hear you when I'm fluxed,

so don't go saying anything you don't want me to hear."

They promised.

"You'll do it, then?" Willa asked. "You'll flux when we get to the gym?"

"Fine," Bax said, his cheeks turning red.

Suddenly, his face clouded over. "Oh, no," he said, and *boom*! He fluxed into a rock that instant, landing heavily on the hall floor.

They all stared.

"Oops," Marigold finally said.

"What part of *when we get to the gym* did he not understand?" Willa grumbled.

Sebastian felt sorry for Rock-Bax. "You know he fluxes by accident all the time." Why did no one in this class understand the others' magic properly?

Marigold bit her lip. "Should we take him to Nurse Riley?"

"No," Sebastian replied. "We need to all stay together. Just get the wheelbarrow and we'll take him with us." Did they not remember the rules, either?

"Ugh," Willa groaned. "Okay."

Marigold laughed. "At least he didn't turn into a piano."

Once Rock-Bax was in the wheelbarrow, Marigold read out the next item on the scavenger hunt list: *An invisible autograph*. "This one is unfair," she said. "Typical Flickers can just sign their names and then make the signatures disappear."

Sebastian was the only Flicker on their team, but since his magic was upside down, he couldn't make anyone's signature disappear. However . . .

"I have an idea," he said. "Let's go to the Flicker classroom. There is so much invisible stuff in there. I'm sure I can find an invisible permission slip or something with a signature on it."

"Perfect. Let's go!" Willa cried. She grabbed Marigold's hand, and they ran down the hall.

Sebastian picked up the handles of the wheelbarrow. Oof, it was heavy. By the time they all reached the Flicker classroom, his arms hurt almost as much as his head.

The room was empty. Well, empty of other fifth graders. And to Willa and Marigold, it no doubt looked clean and orderly. Rock-Bax didn't have eyes, but if he had, the room would've looked tidy to him, too.

Sebastian, on the other hand, saw that it was chock-full of invisible pencils, invisible books, invisible Dreggs, and invisible boogers. In the back of the room were the remains of someone's invisible lunch.

It was very messy, but at least it was quiet.

"Well?" Marigold said.

Sebastian shuffled through the invisible papers in the trash can by the teacher's desk. He found a note that had been signed by a parent and held it aloft. "Here we go."

"Really?" Willa said.

"Really," Sebastian said. "If Coach needs proof, he can ask a Flicker to turn it visible again."

"Hooray!" cried Willa.

"Like Bax said, you're a secret weapon," Marigold added.

Ghost peeked her head out of Sebastian's pocket. "Cool magic," she squeaked. "Let me know if you see any invisible cheese in here, will you?"

Sebastian laughed, and with the invisible autograph done, they turned their attention to the next clue.

11

The Paste-Eaters had used up a lot of time finding *ghost*, so it was a good thing Nory had paid attention in science class. She knew that four pounds on the moon would be at least twenty-four pounds on Earth.

There was a big hanging scale in the science lab, so they ran there from the library.

They weighed some beakers. And Elliott's boots. And the biggest textbook they could find.

Sigh. Everything was too light.

While they were working, Elliott told them all about the Flare lab at Sage Academy. He said it had tall tables like a science lab, but high ceilings like an airplane hangar or something. He talked about hex gloves and special equipment. And he was very excited to study with Sage's "amazing" Flare teacher, Dr. Vogel.

Ugh! Nory did not want to hear about Dr. Vogel. Didn't Elliott remember that he was more of a Freezer than a Flare? That he was a UDM kid?

Apparently not, since now he was all "Flare this" and "Flare that." And Pepper kept *listening*, asking Elliott questions, like she was happy for Elliott to go away to boarding school.

Nory plopped a microscope on the scale.

Nope. It only weighed six pounds.

She plopped a beaker on the scale.

One pound.

"My brickpack!" Andres cried just as Elliott was telling Pepper about the special student kitchen Sage had for Flares studying cooking techniques. "It holds six bricks," said Andres, "and those are about four and a half pounds each. So it's twenty-seven pounds."

"Perfect!" Nory cried. "Done." She glanced at the list. "Next thing is a lemon. Let's go to the cafeteria."

"A lemon?" Elliott asked as they all followed Nory down the hall. "I thought we needed *an invisible signature*."

"We do," she explained. "We can use lemon juice for invisible ink."

"Oh, yeah," Pepper said. "We sign a name with lemon juice on paper. Then when we show it to Coach, Elliott will flare just a little bit under the paper, and the heat will make the lemon juice turn brown. It works."

"I guess we can do that," Elliott said. "Sounds fun."

"Great," said Nory, glad he was focused on something besides Dr. Vogel and the Flare kitchen. "But we have to hurry. Only twenty-five minutes left."

● ● ●

There was no fresh fruit in the cafeteria. None. Just saltines in little packets, ketchup in little packets, and salt in little packets.

"Do you remember how Sage has that salad bar with piles of strawberries and pineapple?" Elliott said. "I mean, think how much fruit you would eat if it was always strawberries and pineapple instead of apples and more apples, like we get here?"

A lump formed in Nory's throat. There he was, going on about Sage again. Didn't he see that it hurt her feelings when he talked like that?

Pepper grabbed Nory's arm. "I have an idea," she cried. "Carrot!"

"We don't have carrots in this cafeteria," Nory said. "Just packets."

"No, Carrot the bunny. She has a stash of fruit and veggies in Ms. Starr's desk. Remember how she was eating broccoli before? Maybe she has a lemon!"

And off they ran.

• • •

Carrot did have a lemon. But . . . she was not about to part with it.

"You know," she said as the Paste-Eaters clustered around her, "I was a gigantic help to the other UDM team."

"That's cool," said Pepper. "And we're so excited you're giving us your lemon."

"Not so fast."

"Not so fast?"

"Well," said Carrot, "do you know what the other team did to say thank you?"

"Did they say *thank you*?" Elliott deadpanned.

"Yes. But they also changed their team name to Friends of Carrot." The bunny preened, stroking her whiskers. "What will you change *your* name to if I give you my lemon?"

Nory loved the name Paste-Eaters. It showed their togetherness, and how they all liked the same music.

Carrot tilted her head. "I see you're hesitating," she said. "But you and the other UDM team, plus various Fuzzies I know from around school—people have been coming in here all night, wanting my help. *Carrot, do you have any heels of lettuce? Carrot, do you have any ghosts? Carrot, can we carry you around so we have a lucky rabbit's foot?*"

"Yes, but—" Pepper started.

"I have to look out for my own interests," Carrot said. "So pay the price or I keep my lemon."

Pepper looked at her team. "I think we should take this deal."

"Fine," Andres said. "Instead of the Paste-Eaters, we can be the *Carrot*-Eaters."

Carrot gave him a look. "Ha-ha, and *no*."

Nory decided they *should* change their team name. They needed that lemon. "How about Carrot's Team?"

"Or Carrot's Connections," said Pepper.

The bunny looked doubtful.

"Carrot's Kids," tried Nory.

"Carrot Is Cool?" said Elliott.

"Change your name to . . . Carrot's Number One Fans," Carrot said. "Then you can have the lemon."

Ugh, Nory did *not* like that name. But, okay, whatever. "We have less than twenty-two minutes left," she told her teammates.

Twenty-two minutes to get the last items. To stay upbeat. To show Elliott how special Dunwiddle was. To make him remember how important friendship was so he'd forget about pineapples and Dr. Vogel. To win that secret room and win back Elliott at the same time. "So let's do it," Nory added. "We are now officially Carrot's Fans."

"Carrot's *Number One* Fans," Carrot corrected.

"Yes, fine, Carrot's Number One Fans!" Nory cried. She scratched out *Paste-Eaters* on the top of the page and wrote the new name. "Can we have the lemon now?"

"Why, yes, you may," said Carrot. "Here you go." She tossed Nory a small, slightly bruised lemon.

It was a sad lemon. But it would do.

Nory peeled the lemon. Then she squeezed it and used a paintbrush to sign her name on a piece of blank paper. *Elinor Boxwood Horace*, invisible now—but not forever. Done.

"Bye, Carrot," said Elliott, lingering at the door of the UDM classroom. "You know, I'll miss you when I go to Sage Academy."

"Ooh," said Carrot. "I hear they have a skunk garden."

"They do," said Elliott, giving a thumbs-up. "And a greenhouse for growing vegetables, too."

"Maybe I can come visit you and see the tomato plants," said Carrot wistfully. "Dunwiddle's winter tomatoes are really bland. They're hardly tomatoes at all."

"Elliott!" snapped Nory. "Do you want to win, or do you want to stand around discussing the tomatoes of Sage Academy?"

"Sorry," said Elliott. "I'm just—it's my last chance to talk to Carrot. I thought she'd be interested."

"I am," said Carrot.

Nory dug her fingernails into her palms. "Can we

please just go?" she said. "We have to find *something forty years old.*"

"Run, Carrot's Number One Fans, run!" called out Carrot as she waved her little paw goodbye.

Something forty years old.

Andres had an idea, so Nory's team zoomed down the hall, up the stairs, down another hall, around a corner, past the art room and around another corner, to a hall lined with pictures.

There were framed photographs on the wall. Each one showed eighth graders in graduation robes.

"We need one from forty years ago," Andres said, from the ceiling.

Nory counted backward through the photos. "Twenty years ago . . . twenty-five . . . thirty . . . thirty-five . . . forty. There we are."

"Fantastic!" said Andres. "The picture is forty years old."

Nory studied the students in the photo. Pepper leaned in to look, too.

"Their hairdos were funny back then," said Pepper. "So old-fashioned."

"We'll be up on the wall one day, too," Nory said.

Pepper nodded. "I can't imagine being an eighth grader, though."

Nory couldn't quite imagine it, either. But she *could* imagine how proud she'd feel, graduating from Dunwiddle.

As Pepper lifted the photo off its nail, Nory turned to Elliott meaningfully. "We'll be the first ever graduating Upside-Down Magic class," she said.

Elliott nodded.

"Ms. Starr will be so proud," continued Nory. "Don't you want to be on the wall with us?"

"I mean, sure, but . . ." He shrugged uncomfortably.

"It will be *very special*," said Nory. "Just like Dunwiddle is *very special*. Think about it. 'Kay?"

"Think about what?"

"How special we are," Nory told him. "'Cause all night you've been like, Sage Academy this, and Sage Academy that, and *Oooh, vegetable garden*, when you don't even care about vegetables. And *Ooh, what a great Flare lab*, without even thinking about how there won't be any Freezer studies there, because Sage doesn't have upside-down-magic classes, period. Extra skunks in a garden don't make a school awesome. Extra *books* don't make a school awesome!"

"Nory—"

"PEOPLE make a school awesome," Nory interrupted. "Other kids with upside-down magic make a school awesome, especially if you, yourself, have upside-down magic—which you do. Do you remember when you and I tried to do the box of normal?"

Elliott blinked. "Of course I do."

"Well, guess what? Sage Academy is one enormous box of normal. 'Normal' is what they do there!"

"Nory, come on," Elliott said. "Sage has a lot to offer me. Don't you want me to at least have the chance to see what that could be?"

Nory lifted her chin. "Dunwiddle is public. It's free for *everyone*. And it's where we do UDM. Here is where we're allowed to be our true selves, and Dunwiddle—*not* Sage—is where your best friends are."

"You're not being fair," snapped Elliott.

Pepper touched Nory's arm. "Nory," she said softly, "both schools are great in different ways. Elliott is excited for Sage. We shouldn't spoil it for him."

Nory jerked away. Why was Pepper taking Elliott's side?

She felt her skin prick. *Uh-oh.*

Blood rushed to face and fingers and toes, and her body began to transform.

She grew whiskers. *Whoosh!*

And suckers. *Sloop sloop!*

And paws. *Pa-thud!*

Now she was Squippy-Nory, puppy in the front and squid at the back. Her tentacles rippled and made sucking sounds on the floor.

"Zamboozle," said Andres.

"Omigosh," said Elliott. He sounded dismayed but also exasperated. "I didn't mean to make her flux. I swear."

"Can I pick you up?" Pepper asked, bending over. "I'm pausing my magic, okay?"

Squippy-Nory nodded. Pepper picked her up, and Squippy-Nory hid her face in Pepper's neck.

She couldn't look at Elliott. She was too mad and embarrassed and . . . squiggly.

"Shh, Nory," said Pepper softly. "You've got to calm down, okay? You've got to calm down and flux back, because we have only one item left on the list—and only ten minutes to find it."

Nory felt out of sorts even after she fluxed back into her human self. In her squippy form, she'd licked Pepper's neck. She'd flailed her tentacles about, and one of them had landed in Elliott's hair. She'd been out of control.

No one was making a big deal about it. But still, she felt humiliated, especially when it came to Elliott. (A *tentacle*! In his *hair*!)

And he'd said she wasn't being fair. Well, he wasn't being fair, either. So there.

She made a show of consulting the list as she

walked with Pepper and Elliott down the hall. Andres flew above them. "We need *a member of a royal family*," Nory said in a tight, formal voice.

"Royal carriage. Royal scepter. Royal corgis," said Elliott, brainstorming.

"Think prince. Or princess," said Pepper. "*Member of a royal family.*"

"Royal icing?" deadpanned Elliott. "Royal blue?"

"King or queen," said Pepper. "Prince. Princess."

How about something that ends in *king*?" said Andres. "Like, I don't know, joking? Puking? Biking?"

"No one's going to puke," said Pepper dryly. "Besides, I don't think that would count."

Ah. Nory had it. She almost didn't want to have it, because she wanted to brood silently. "The chess set in Ms. Starr's room," she announced through a clenched jaw. "It has a king and a queen."

They ran back to Ms. Starr's classroom, and Nory grabbed the chess set's queen.

"We have all ten items," Elliott said, grinning and holding up his hand.

Nory slapped his palm, but the high five felt stiff. What did it matter if they had all ten things if she and Elliott weren't behaving like best friends on the one night they had together? Did that mean that they weren't best friends after all?

And if they weren't best friends, what did *anything* matter?

12

There were eight minutes left for Sebastian's team to find the final two items.

For *something forty years old,* they couldn't agree. Marigold suggested the pretty silver hair clip she was wearing, which belonged to her grandmother. "It's super old," she said. "Like from when she was a kid."

"But that's not forty years old *exactly,*" said Sebastian.

"It doesn't say *exactly forty,*" said Willa. "Just *forty.*"

"I think exactly forty is what it means, though."

"Come on," said Willa, looking at the clock. "I bet Coach will accept it."

"I'm sure stuff the other teams bring won't have proof of age," said Marigold. "And this is obviously, like, ancient."

"I think we need proof of age," said Sebastian. "Like if we had a magazine from forty years ago with the date on it, or—"

"Sebastian!" Willa exploded. "Stop overanalyzing. The hair clip is fine!"

The sound waves of her loud voice seemed to slam into his forehead.

Sebastian gave up.

He didn't want to argue anymore. He did want to win the secret room, but he couldn't push his point and have Willa keep screeching. "All right," he said. "Hair clip."

The last clue for Friends of Carrot was *a member of a royal family.*

"There are decks of cards in the library," Marigold said. "We'll get a queen or king."

Sebastian liked her solution, and he was always

up for going to the library. So quiet. He pushed the wheelbarrow with Rock-Bax through the door and took a deep breath. Ah, silence. He lifted his goggles and touched where the rubber chafed his skin.

Marigold found a deck immediately, chose the king of diamonds, and ran right out the library door. "Two minutes left!" she called out. "Let's go!" Willa followed.

Sebastian put his goggles back in place. He picked up the wheelbarrow and sighed. Ghost peeked her head out of his pocket. "Why do you always have to push the wheelbarrow?"

"I don't know."

"Doesn't seem fair," Ghost squeaked.

Nope, Sebastian thought. *It's not.*

Sebastian turned the wheelbarrow around, opened the library door, and backed out. Then he angled the wheelbarrow forward again.

"Come *on*, Sebastian!" Willa called, making him wince. "We want to *win*, remember?"

He wanted to yell back, *I do, actually. But do* you

remember me? *Can you think about* me *for two seconds?* Still, he pushed ahead, the rumbling sounds of the wheelbarrow banging into his head with every step.

Nory's team was waiting to hand their objects over to Coach. Andres had his brickpack on so that he could stand among them.

Coach, back in human form, did a lot of nodding and humming as he noted each team's accomplishments. Ms. Starr, Nurse Riley, and the other teachers were there as well. They checked off items as kids brought them in.

Nory spotted Sebastian, Willa, and Marigold as they joined the line. But where was Bax? Oh. In his wheelbarrow. She hoped that was on purpose.

"Hey, Nory," Elliott said, stepping closer. "Want to hear a joke?"

Nory stiffened. If he wanted to be nice to her, he should tell her she was right about Dunwiddle and how it was better than Sage. That's what she wanted to hear, not a joke.

Elliott went on anyway. "What's the difference between a puppy and a flea?"

"I don't know," she muttered.

"A puppy can have fleas, but a flea can't have puppies. Get it? Ha!" He laughed loudly, but it wasn't his normal laugh. It was his trying-too-hard laugh.

"Don't joke about flea puppies," she said. "I might turn into one."

He bumped his shoulder against hers. "Ohh, a fluppy! Would you be a puppy the size of a flea, or would you be big and have flea legs?"

"I'd prefer not to flux again today. My squippy was embarrassing enough," she said.

"Oh, come on. You didn't even piddle."

Nory swallowed. She was finding it harder and harder to stay mad at Elliott. "Well, the night is still young," she said grudgingly.

He laughed, a real laugh this time. "You know, I'm glad there was a storm and I didn't go to the concert at Sage." He looked at her earnestly. "And I'm glad we get to have Big Night together."

Aw, Elliott.

She wanted to forgive him, and here he was, making it so easy to forgive him . . .

And so she did. "Yeah, yeah, good stuff," she said.

"You know what you need?" he asked.

She smiled. "What?"

"More sugar!" he said. He handed her another moon cookie from behind his back, wrapped in a napkin.

"You moon cookie hoarder," Nory said as she took it. "We would be seriously fainting from lack of snacks without you."

"Carrot's Number One Fans," Coach yelled. "Bring me your items!"

Nory's heart sped up as her team handed Coach all the things on the list. Well, they didn't hand over Andres. They just let him float up on his leash and pointed out the highness of his heels.

Coach chuckled. "Very clever," he said.

"Yup, yup, yup," he said as he ran through the rest of their items. "All approved. Move to the side, team."

They'd done it. They'd found all ten!

"So are we going to win?" Elliott asked.

"We are absolutely going to win," Nory said, bouncing on the balls of her feet.

The gym was packed and loud. The sound waves were very, very bright. Sebastian was completely overwhelmed.

He should get his head cone. He *would* get his head cone, just as soon as Coach was done checking off their items. Even though he knew his friends wouldn't want him to wear it.

Their team took a step closer, and Ghost stuck her head out of Sebastian's pocket. "Are we almost done? I don't like it here."

Pepper was nearby, chatting with Nory and Elliott. Sebastian wondered if Ghost, in part, was feeling the unpleasant effects of her fiercing magic. "It won't be much longer, I promise," he told the mouse. "And thank you so much for doing this. You're being super brave."

Finally it was their turn. Coach looked over their

items, peeking into Sebastian's hoodie pocket to hear Ghost say her name. After the Flicker teacher flickered the permission slip into visibility, Coach smiled and gave them full points.

Sebastian was glad. They actually might win the secret room! But all the same, he felt the judging was a little lax. He couldn't believe they'd gotten points for *something forty years old* by using Willa's grandmother's hair clip. He *really* couldn't believe that so many of the other teams had gotten points for *roll* by bringing in hamburger buns.

Coach wrote a large ten on their team's checklist and attached it to his clipboard. "Move along, then. Well done!"

Willa started jumping. "We got ten!" she cried, grabbing Marigold's arm.

Marigold started jumping, too. "We got *ten!*" she squealed.

"If more than one team has the same number of points, how will they decide the winner?" Willa wondered.

"Wait and see," said Coach. "Now, move along."

More jumping. More squealing. Tens and hundreds of squeaks on the gym floor. Hundreds and thousands of voices. *Aaargh!*

Sebastian pushed the wheelbarrow over to Nurse Riley. "Bax is a rock. Can you help him flux back?"

"You bet," Nurse Riley said. "Hey, Bax, nice to see you using your magic to help your team. I'll get you sorted out in no time." He took the wheelbarrow and headed off.

The UDM camp area was yards away from Coach, the scoring platform, and the throngs of excited fifth graders. Even so, it was plenty loud. Sebastian knelt and started searching for his duffel bag, where his cone was packed. His head hurt so much, it was hard to focus.

WOOOOOONNNGGG! Coach blew the air horn.

And again.

And again.

Sebastian finally found his duffel. He pulled out his head cone and put it on.

Ahhh. That was a little better.

"Ghost, you can take off now," he said, holding open his hoodie pocket and peering down at the mouse.

Ghost wiggled. "I'm afraid to come out. It is so loud."

Sebastian checked to make sure Pepper was far away. "It's okay. You're safe. And you'll feel tons better as soon as you're out of the gym."

"Would you mind dropping me at one of the air vents?" said the mouse. "That'll give me a straight shot to the teachers' lounge. That place has great cracker crumbs."

Sebastian walked Ghost to the air vents, squatted down, and set Ghost on the floor. "Thank you for your help," he said.

"And thank you for the string cheese." Ghost's little eyes widened. "Oh. You're wearing a lampshade."

"It's a cone," Sebastian explained. "To stop the noise. I know it looks odd."

"It doesn't look *that* odd," Ghost said. "No stranger

than other things humans wear. Like baseball hats. Or belts. I mean, really. Belts?"

"I don't like belts, either," said Sebastian. "Travel safe and I'll see you soon, okay?"

"Yup, yup. Take care," said Ghost. "Bye!"

The mouse scurried into the air vent and was gone.

Sebastian rejoined his teammates, who were watching Coach on the platform. Coach gestured toward a whiteboard. On it was a chart with all the team names and scores. Quite a few teams had ten points. So who was going to win?

Willa and Marigold clutched each other. Nory grabbed Elliott's arm. Even Bax, now back in human form, looked excited.

"And now," Coach announced, "the *real* scoring begins!"

13

Nory gasped. What did Coach mean, "the *real* scoring"? And why did he say it with that eyebrow wiggle? And that sly grin?

"Pepper, what's going on?" she whispered.

Pepper pointed at Coach, who stood at the whiteboard scrawling lines through totals and replacing them with new scores. "Deductions," she whispered back. "He's giving out deductions."

Nory felt dizzy.

"Where are the Sparkies?" Coach asked. "Sparkies, raise your hands."

Lacey Clench and her friends nervously raised their hands.

Coach consulted his notes. "I see here that a member of the Sparkies called people *losers, wonkos, weirdos,* and *tragic failures.*" He regarded Lacey with disappointment. "Nothing wrong with a little competitive spirit. But name-calling and rude insults are *not* competitive spirit."

"It was a joke," Lacey protested.

Coach held up a warning finger. "Wrong," he said. "Rule number one is *Use common courtesy.* Two points off." He slashed a line through the Sparkies' score, changing it from a ten to an eight.

"Two points off for a joke?" Lacey cried.

Up on the platform, Ms. Starr cleared her throat. "The decision of the judges is final."

Lacey kicked the gym floor.

"Moving on," said Coach. "Where can I find the Unseeables?"

Four Flickers raised their hands. Their expressions were guilty.

"You made another team's bread roll invisible and then stole it," Coach said disapprovingly.

"That was you, Anastasia?" Princess cried. "You stole our roll?"

"Rule number five: *Cheating or stealing will get you kicked out of the game*," Coach said.

Alarm and excitement rippled through the crowd.

"Anastasia's the strongest Flicker in our grade," Elliott whispered. "And now she's kicked out!"

Three of the four naughty Flickers disappeared from sight. Anastasia turned invisible except for her head, which she bowed in shame.

"Kicked out," Nory said under her breath. "Holy zamboozle in a jar!"

The deductions continued. Some teams lost two points, some lost four. One team lost eight.

So far the other UDM team was the only one who had kept all ten points. Even though Bax, Sebastian, Marigold, and Willa were her competition, Nory still felt a swell of pride for her UDM friends.

"And last, Carrot's Number One Fans," Coach announced.

They raised their hands.

Coach looked at his notes. "Nory Horace—" He paused and lifted his eyes.

Nory's throat went dry.

"Nory, you acquired my stamp on your own," Coach said. "Without your teammates. And rule number three clearly states, *Teams have to collect all scavenger hunt items together.*" Coach crossed off the beautiful ten. He replaced it with an eight.

"Nooooo!" Nory wailed.

Pepper leaned over. "It's not your fault," she said softly.

"Yes it *is*," Nory cried, wishing she, too, could disappear. "I lost this whole game for our team. Me."

Pepper patted her arm.

"Listen up, kids," Coach announced. "You may think we are finished with this scavenger hunt. But you're wrong. Because now, my friends, it is time for—dum, dum, dum—the final challenge!"

Nory's jaw fell open. The *final* challenge?

Coach waved a stack of notecards. "The final challenge is for each team to find three new items."

"Even us?" Anastasia's head said.

"Every team except the Unseeables," Coach corrected.

Anastasia pouted. Then the lower half of her face turned invisible. Now she was just a forehead and a pair of eyebrows.

"Here's what's going to happen," Coach explained. "Each team will be given a clue for item number one. Once you find item one, come turn it in. Then you learn what item number two is. When you have item two, turn that in and get the clue for item three. Each item is worth five points. The challenge is over when the first team successfully turns in the third item."

"And then you add up the points again?" Nory asked.

"Exactly," Coach said.

Nory did some quick math. If they were the first to find all three items, they would get fifteen points.

Add that to the eight points they had now, and they would have twenty-three.

$$8 + 15 = 23$$

If that happened, Sebastian's team, starting with ten points, would only get ten final challenge points, for a total of twenty points.

$$10 + 10 = 20$$

Twenty-three beat twenty. Nory's team *could* win!

"Teams, are you ready?" Coach said.

"Yes!" roared everyone except for the Unseeables. Anastasia disappeared entirely with a *pop*.

14

"Y our head cone," Willa said to Sebastian as Marigold went up to get the first clues of the final challenge. "Are you going to keep wearing it even when we go back to scavenger hunting?"

"Yes."

"Just because, you know, I, ah—" Willa glanced anxiously at Lacey Clench and her team.

"I'm wearing my head cone and my goggles," said Sebastian, making an effort to keep his voice calm. "My magic is stronger than it used to be. I need them both now."

"I just don't want you to trip or anything," said Willa.

"I don't comment on what *you're* wearing, Willa," Sebastian said through gritted teeth.

Marigold ran to them, holding a slip of paper. "We need to find *something sticky*!" she cried. "Let's go. This is easy!"

Everyone in the gym was screaming and laughing as their teams set off. Everyone was running, too, which made wave after wave of sound rise from the floor. "Tape," Willa said, over the hubbub. "We can get some in the art room."

The four of them ran down the hall and into the art room, where Willa opened the supply cupboard and pulled out a roll of masking tape.

"Done!" she said, smiling.

"Back to the gym," Willa said.

Back to the gym? Ugh.

Of course they had to go back to the gym.

Reluctantly, Sebastian followed his teammates. His eyes stung. His head pounded. He didn't think he could last much longer.

"Something sticky," Nory read aloud. They were back in this game, and she was not going to let them lose. No way.

"Gum," said Elliott. "Does anyone have gum?"

"Is gum even sticky?" Pepper asked.

"When it's being chewed," Elliott and Nory said at the same time.

"I think I have some in my locker," Andres said.

The four of them ran to the row of UDM lockers. Andres rummaged through his, but came up with nothing. "No, no, no," he said.

Nory opened her own locker to see if she had any gum.

Nope.

Pepper searched her locker, too.

"Oh!" she cried, lifting something orange into the air. "An old gummy unicorn in my jacket pocket. And it is super, super sticky."

"Yes!" cheered Elliott.

"Don't eat it," warned Nory.

"I'm not going to eat it," Pepper said. "It has a nickel stuck to it. And a piece of hair."

"Okay, then," said Nory. "We're right on track. Back to the gym."

Sebastian did some deep breathing as their team handed Coach the tape. So many voices in the gym. Kids running one way, kids running the other. He needed to rest his eyes.

"Good job," Coach told them. He lifted the air horn to his lips.

"Nooooooo!" Sebastian begged, but it was too late. Coach was blowing it less than a foot away from him. The intense sound wave slammed into Sebastian.

"Congratulations. You're the first team to get item number one," Coach said. "Here's a clue for number two." He handed Marigold an index card.

"We're in the lead," said Willa.

Sebastian looked at the other groups who had lined up to show their sticky things to Coach. A

Fuzzy team had brought in a slug. Another Fuzzy team had a terrarium in which a spider was making a web. The Sparkies had melted an old sneaker so that its glue oozed out. Behind them, a team of Flickers held . . . a stick?

No. Coach would not accept a stick for *sticky*. No way.

"*A nonhuman pyramid,*" Marigold said, reading from the new index card. "Any ideas?"

Coach accepted the slug as sticky. *WOOOOOONNNGGG!* Air horn!!!!

"What about Legos?" Willa asked. "We could build a pyramid with them. Do we have Legos in our class?"

"No, we don't," Marigold said.

Coach accepted the spiderweb as well. *WOOOOOONNNGGG!* Air horn!!!!

"I know. Bax can flux into a pyramid," Willa cried.

"Not happening," said Bax. "I don't do pyramid."

"But you *could*," Willa said.

"I can do five objects," said Bax. "Rock, piano,

leash, swivel chair, and rain poncho. None are pyramid-shaped."

"You could at least try," Willa cajoled. "It would only be for a minute."

Did Willa pay attention to anyone else's magic? Ever?

"Willa!" snapped Bax. "I can't do pyramid. I. Do. Not. Know. How. Why are we even still talking about this?"

"I just thought—"

"It's like me telling you to just rain outdoors," Bax said. "Can you do that, Willa? Just for a minute? Huh?"

"Oh," said Willa, finally getting it. "No."

Sebastian watched Coach touch the melted shoe, nod, and *WOOOOOONNNGGG!* Air horn!!!!

Sebastian saw the Flickers hand over their stick.

"Ooh," Marigold said. "There's that marble pyramid statue just inside the side entrance, with the inspirational quote thing. Let's go."

Coach looked at the stick. And then . . . air horn! *WOOOOOONNNGGG!*

Sebastian. Was. Dying. The air horn was unbearable, and the stick should not have been approved. "Why, why, why?" he cried.

"What are you talking about?" Bax asked.

"Coach okayed the stick." Sebastian shook his aching head. "It's not fair to people who actually found sticky stuff."

"Forget it," Marigold said. "We have to get to the pyramid before the others."

"Carrot's Number One Fans," Coach finally said. "You're up."

Pepper showed him the unicorn gummy.

Coach poked it cautiously. "Yes," he said. "That is definitely sticky."

He blew the air horn. Hurrah! And handed them the second clue.

Sebastian read the quote beneath the marble pyramid statue. It said, *Anything is possible.* He liked that idea, but he wasn't sure it was true.

Three teams of kids were trying to heave it off the platform where it sat. But the statue was too heavy.

"It's too big," one kid moaned. "No one can move it."

"No one except the Friends of Carrot," Marigold said, grinning.

She placed her hand on the pyramid statue and closed her eyes.

The pyramid quivered.

It wobbled.

Then it shrank to the size of an apple.

"Where'd it go?" a Fluxer cried.

Marigold caught the tiny pyramid as it dropped. "Sorry not sorry," she told the other teams.

Sebastian gave her a thumbs-up, and they were off. *We might win this*, Sebastian thought. *Marigold's a secret weapon, too.*

Nory's team was stuck on *nonhuman pyramid*.

"Does anyone have a cheese grater?" Elliott asked. "That's pyramid-shaped."

"Why would anyone bring a cheese grater to

Big Night?" Andres asked. "It's not like we all grate cheese together before the paper owls."

"Okay, fine," said Elliott. "Just brainstorming."

"Could we make a pyramid out of Popsicle sticks?" wondered Andres.

"That would take too long, with the glue having to dry and everything," said Pepper.

"What about Magna-Tiles?" Nory said. "Can we find Magna-Tiles somewhere?"

"I just realized," cried Elliott, bouncing on his toes.

"What?" asked Nory.

"I've totally got this," Elliott said happily.

"You do?" Nory asked.

"I do!"

They followed him back to the gym. There were only a couple teams lined up for *nonhuman pyramid*, Nory noticed. It was much harder than *something sticky*.

The Sparkies were first. They handed in a pyramid flared out of wood. It looked pretty good, Nory had to admit. Burned, but definitely a perfect pyramid shape.

Next, Sebastian's team handed in a marble pyramid—oh, it was the one from the front hall. Marigold had shrunk it!

Both solutions were accepted, and both teams were given the third and final clue.

Elliott waited silently, focusing on his magic. Nory was sure he planned to make an ice pyramid, but he had only made objects of ice from thin air a couple times. It wasn't easy. Could he manage it?

Finally, it was their turn. Nory's heart beat faster, but Elliott walked confidently up to Coach, knelt on the floor, and—

Zap! Zap!

Zap! Zap!

Floop!

He made five sheets of ice, four triangles and a square, then—

Clang!

He iced them together to make a perfect pyramid.

"Excellent work," Coach bellowed. "Outstanding." He blew the air horn.

Nory loved that air horn. Could she get an air horn of her own at home? Maybe Coach would let her borrow it.

"Here you go," Coach said to them, handing Elliott an index card. "The final clue."

15

Sebastian read the last clue to his teammates as they huddled in one corner of the gym: *"Something no one has ever seen before."*

"How are we supposed to find that?" asked Marigold.

"It's too hard," said Bax.

Sebastian knew that if they found this item fast, they would be first. They would win.

"Can I shrink something again?" wondered Marigold. "No one has ever seen a tiny sleeping bag."

Sebastian shook his head. "People *have* seen tiny sleeping bags," he said. "For dolls or whatever."

Marigold wrinkled her brow. "What about tiny backpacks?"

"Same thing."

"We have to think beyond shrinkage," Bax said. "What's something no one has ever seen before?"

Sebastian's head was still pounding, and his eyes were still burning. The cone wasn't big enough to block all the noise.

"Sebastian," Marigold said. "You can be our answer. You see invisible things."

"But I can't bring the things I see to Coach," said Sebastian. "We can't hand in a sound wave."

Marigold tilted her head. "We brought in the signature."

"That was an invisible piece of paper," Sebastian said. Did he really have to explain this? "It was flickered visible."

"Let's bring in a fart," said Marigold. "You'd see that, right, Sebastian? If it's loud?"

"I *just said* we can't hand in a sound wave."

"No, we'd, like, save up the fart and then let it out in front of Coach," Marigold explained. "That way you'd see it."

"It's hard to fart on command," Bax said thoughtfully. "I could burp again, though."

"No," said Sebastian. "I've seen farts. I've seen burps. We can't win with any of those. They won't count for points."

He knew he was doing that "analyzing thing" that Willa hated, but he couldn't just let them make a totally ordinary burp or fart sound, have him say he'd seen it, and lose the game. He was looking out for *them*, for their team!

His head thumped. Thumped. Thumped.

"Guys, we have to figure something out," Marigold said. She gestured at the other teams who were huddled together. "They're on the final clue, too."

Willa gripped Sebastian's arm. "I know. We'll bring you. Your eyeballs. Inside of you, of course. Your *eyeballs* have seen things no one has ever seen!"

Oh, her shouting!

Sebastian didn't think he could stay patient for much longer. "One: Everyone has already seen my eyeballs, so we won't get points. Two: The things my eyeballs have seen *have* been seen by someone, and that someone is me! And finally: I am a member of our team, Friends of Carrot. I am not an object to be brought in."

"I was an object," Bax said. "I was an object, and I couldn't even talk. I didn't even have *limbs*. And I didn't get to help with the last three clues."

"Yeah," said Willa to Sebastian. "Bax had to take yucky medicine to get back to his boy self. But he didn't complain. So why won't you just let us bring your eyeballs?"

"Because I don't think we'll win with my eyeballs."

Willa frowned. "It would be so *fun* to bring you in."

WOOOOOOOONG! "Will the air horn ever stop?" Sebastian moaned.

"Yes," Willa said. "When we bring you in as thing three!"

"No!"

"Listen," Marigold said. "Do you remember when we were at Sage Academy and you won the hide-and-seek?"

"Yeah." That had been a great night. Nowhere near so loud as this one, since the building was so large, with nearly soundproof stone walls. And Sebastian had found every single invisible Flicker, within minutes. It had been a triumph.

"You played the game your way and guess what happened?"

"We won."

"Yes, but you ruined the whole night for all the Sage Academy kids," Marigold said. "No one got to do any seeking except you. It was nice for us UDM kids to win, but everyone else was upset. People were so mad at you the next day, they threw spitballs."

Technically, it was only one spitball. But yes, Sebastian remembered it.

"The point is, we don't *know* if your eyeballs would count or not," Marigold said. She took a moment, then softened her tone and said, "But they might. And we all think it would be fun. We won't know unless we try, and you're just—you're missing the 'having fun' part of the point of this whole thing, kind of like you did at Sage Academy's hide-and-seek. We're just asking you to *adapt a little*, Sebastian, and see it from our point of view."

Sebastian knew Marigold was trying to be nice.

But when she said *adapt a little*, he exploded. "Adapt a little?" he said. "Adapt a little? What do you think I do all day, every day? You guys are super loud, all the time. You sing off-key for no reason, you bang on your desks, you shout. No one in this whole school ever says, 'Let's have a quiet hour so Sebastian's head and eyes won't hurt.' No one says, 'Let's all remember not to slam our desks closed,' or 'Let's not wear loud, heavy boots,' or 'Let's whisper for at least some part of the school day because our friend Sebastian's eyeballs feel like they're salty and burning when we scream all the time.' No. I'm the one who has to wear goggles, all day every day, and when I wear my head cone because I'm actually in pain, you want me to take it off. You want me to *adapt* so I don't make you look uncool or wonky or whatever thing it is that you care about. I am doing stuff all the time to adapt to you guys, because you're my friends. But what do you ever, ever do to make things easier for me?"

His friends looked shocked.

He turned away and marched across the gym. He was done with the scavenger hunt. He was done with his teammates.

He found eye drops in his bag, put them in his eyes, and replaced his cone and goggles.

Then he lay down inside his sleeping bag with his eyes closed and tried not to cry.

16

omething no one has ever seen before," Nory
read aloud. She was fizzy with energy. "If we
get this first, we win."

"Let's go to the hall," Pepper said. "We don't
want any of the other teams hearing our plans and
copying us."

Lacey was standing only a few feet away yelling, "Sparkies! Think harder! How hard is it to find
something's no one's ever seen before?"

Super hard, Nory thought as her team followed
them out the door and to a quiet spot in the hall.

"I could do another ice sculpture?" Elliott suggested when no one could overhear them. Then he shook his head. "No. People have seen ice sculptures."

Pepper turned to Nory. "Oh, wow," she said. "Obvious."

"Obvious what?" Nory said.

"Of course," Andres said, his eyes widening.

"Yah-huh," Elliott said, breaking into a grin.

All three of them stared at her.

"Nory, *you* can win it for us," Elliott explained. "You can flux into a creature no one's ever seen before. The teachers will accept that, no question!"

Nory felt herself glowing. She could be the solution! "Okay, okay, let's think," she said. "It has to be something totally new."

"Flamingo plus kitten," said Andres.

No, that was a kittingo. Nory had done it lots of times.

"Puppy plus bluebird," suggested Pepper.

Done that in tutoring. What was new?

"Could you try fluppy?" asked Elliott.

It was a fun idea, but Nory didn't think she could. The only insect she could manage was mosquito—and adding puppy to something wasn't as easy as adding kitten. "No, I'm pretty sure not."

Omigosh, *owl*! An owl for Big Night. She had to do it.

"Maybe I could add owl to my kitten and do kowl," Nory said. Her words tumbled out. "Nobody's ever seen a kowl before, right?"

"No way, because kowls don't exist," Pepper said. "You'll be the only one."

"Can you do it?" asked Elliott.

Lacey's team burst out of the gym, carrying two jump ropes and a catcher's mitt. "Don't look at us," snapped Lacey. "It's top secret."

The Sparkies were going to have a solution any second. Nory had to focus.

She'd start with owl since that was a new animal for her. "Pepper, pause your magic, okay?"

"Fiercing magic—paused!" said Pepper.

Nory rolled her shoulders and reached inside herself for the part of her that could do birds.

Owl, owl, owl.

She took a deep breath, flapped her arms, and *floof*!

Pop!

Adrenaline rushed through her. She was definitely not her human self, and she was definitely flying. But was she an owl?

Far down the hall, she could see a crumpled piece of paper, sharp as sharp. She could see a tiny spider in the corner of a window. Distance vision.

"You did it," Elliott told her.

"That's our Nory," Pepper said.

"Now just add kitten," Andres told her.

Owl-Nory swooped around. She was strong. She felt carnivorous and alert.

Then, not at all on purpose, *floosh-sh-shh—pop!* Nory fluxed back into her human self, landing on her bottom on the floor.

"Zwingo," she said. "I couldn't hold it."

"Plus you didn't add kitten," Andres pointed out.

"I know."

"Your owl was great," Pepper said. "But Coach has seen owls before."

Lacey and her teammates ran past again, going from one classroom to another. This time they dragged a small carpet behind them. "Only one more step to go," Lacey told the Sparkies. "Hurry!"

Nory scrambled to her feet, more determined than ever. "This time I'll start with kitten," she said. "I can hold kitten longer than my other animals. Maybe if that's my base, I'll be able to do the kowl and keep it?"

With Pepper's magic once again paused, Nory fluxed into a kitten. A black one with tabby stripes. Meow!

Kitten-Nory sat still and groomed her whiskers. She wanted to settle into her shape before trying to add owl.

"Not to push you," said Andres, "but hurry up."

"Mrow-ow," Kitten-Nory told him.

Pop pop! She fluxed, feeling her feet change beneath her.

"No, Nory!" Elliott cried.

What?

"Not koat, *kowl*." Andres said. "We've all seen your koat before!"

Oh, dear. Nory had added goat instead of owl. Now she was an animal with a kitten body and goat ears and legs. Plus a goat mindset.

Ooooh. Koat-Nory spied a lovely bit of yarn hanging off Pepper's sweater.

Yum yum yum! Koat-Nory thought. She'd just have one taste of that yummy yarn.

Nom nom nom.

"No, Nory. Stop." Pepper tried to pry Koat-Nory's teeth from her sweater.

Suddenly, Pepper's magic swooped in. Pepper had un-paused it, distracted by Koat-Nory biting her clothes.

"Baaaaaaaaaaa!" *Pepper was so scary!*

Pop!

"Um, sorry about that," Nory said, back in girl form. She spit out a bit of yarn. "Lost my human mind."

"Start again," said Andres. "Quick!"

A group of Fuzzies passed by holding a teddy bear one of them had brought to the overnight. "Her name is Something No One Else Has Ever Seen Before!" one of them called out proudly. "We just renamed her!"

No way would the teachers accept that solution. Would they?

"Nory," said Elliott, looking her in the eye. "Don't worry about them. You can do this."

Nory took another deep breath. Yes, she could.

Pop pop pop!

She was a tabby kitten.

She focused hard, thinking about how Ms. Starr had taught her that magic was rooted in the feet. She would keep her kitten paws firmly on the ground, rooting down, she decided.

She thought about how Coach had taught her

that bird fluxing involved thinking about your bones, feeling them as you flux, because birds have lighter skeletons than humans.

Then, rooted in the ground and focusing on her skeleton, Nory sprouted lovely wide owl wings.

Go me, she thought. She added a pretty, sleek owl head with a sharp beak, all the while maintaining her kitten legs, tail, and body.

She did it. She was Kowl-Nory. "Hoot-hoot!"

Carrot's Number One Fans sprinted down the hall into the gymnasium. Well, Pepper and Elliott sprinted. Andres ran as fast as he could, his brick-pack bouncing with every step. Kowl-Nory flew.

Could they still win? Had the Fuzzies won with their stuffed bear?

Kowl-Nory hadn't heard the air horn, so she hoped they still had a chance.

Just outside the gymnasium door, the Fuzzies stood dejected, holding their stuffed toy. "I can't believe he didn't give us points for my bear," one of them said.

Yes. Her team *could* still win!

Kowl-Nory swooped into the gym and fluttered down in front of Coach. She extended her fabulous wings so he could see them.

She held her breath.

Coach took one look at her and blew his air horn.

"The final challenge has been accomplished," Coach pronounced.

Elliott, Pepper, and Andres cheered.

Coach took a closer look at Kowl-Nory. "Beautifully done, Nory," he said. "In tutoring, we can work on smoothing out the feather-and-fur combo. I think you might fly more smoothly if you added tail feathers. But you've done a brand-new animal. There's no question that your team has won the final challenge."

Pop pop pop! "Thanks, Coach," Nory said, back in girl form. She shook out her arms. "It wasn't easy."

Coach blew his air horn. "The scavenger hunt is over," he yelled. "And the winning team is . . . Carrot's Number One Fans!"

They'd done it. They'd won. For real, they had won.

"So unfair," Lacey muttered as her team came into the gym. "Obviously, the teachers wanted the UDM kids to win. That task was made for them."

"We thought you'd just solve it by creating a work of art," said Ms. Starr. She spread her upturned palms. "Any of you could have done it."

The grumbling didn't stop, but Nory wasn't bothered.

The secret room was theirs. Nory threw her arms around Elliott.

"We did it!" he said.

"We did," she answered, giving him a squeeze. "Together."

Now her Big Night resolution would succeed. It had to.

17

The scavenger hunt was over. Sebastian heard Coach's announcement.

So he figured he'd stay in the bag. With the covers pulled over his head. Maybe till morning. Why come out? Not only had he lost the secret room, but Willa, Marigold, and Bax were angry at him for refusing to bring in his eyeballs. And for yelling at them.

Plus, he was angry at *them*. Why didn't they care how he felt? Why didn't they care that he was in pain?

"Knock, knock," he heard someone say. "Sebastian?" Marigold, he thought.

Sebastian didn't answer. He didn't want to fight anymore, but if Willa was still cranky and Marigold still didn't understand, he worried that he might yell again.

"We know you're in there," Willa said. "Can you please come talk to us?"

Marigold added, "We're worried about you."

Sebastian steeled himself. Okay, fine. He poked his head out and sat up.

Bax, Marigold, and Willa were kneeling next to him.

"We wondered if we should get Nurse Riley," Bax said.

Sebastian shook his head, making his head cone jiggle a bit. His eyes were feeling a little better, and all Nurse Riley would do was give him the same eye drops he'd already used. "I'm sorry I yelled," he said. Because, suddenly, he was.

Marigold reached out and squeezed his shoulder. "It's all right."

"You were right about your eyeballs," Willa said. "I doubt Coach would have accepted them as item number three." Her voice was soft now. Its waves were fluffy, like cotton candy.

"Also, we wanted to tell you something," Marigold said. She glanced at Willa and Bax, who nodded at her. "You were right about us, too. We *don't* think about ways we could make things easier for you."

Tears welled in Sebastian's eyes. "I just feel . . ." He exhaled. "It's too much, sometimes."

"The noise?" Willa asked.

"Seeing burps?" Bax asked.

"Feeling different?" asked Marigold.

Yes. But it wasn't just that stuff. "My magic is getting stronger," Sebastian explained. "Which means that my headaches are getting stronger. So wearing my goggles isn't enough. I need to wear my head cone, too. I know it embarrasses you all, but I just wish you would think, sometimes, about how it feels to be *me*."

Marigold patted his arm. "We're sorry, Sebastian. So sorry."

"I shouldn't have told you not to wear your cone,"

Willa said, flushing. "Of course you should wear it. Who cares what other people think?"

"Not me, not really," Sebastian said. He tried to be fair. "But our magic can be embarrassing. So I get it about not wanting to, like, add on."

"Stop," Marigold said. "There's a big difference between your magic and ours. We should have seen it, but we didn't." She looked ashamed. "Your magic *hurts*. Ours can be embarrassing, yeah, but it never hurts."

"Mine does," Bax said. "When I flux back. But not like yours."

"We won't shout anymore," Willa said. "Or we'll try not to."

"And maybe can make some quiet periods in class," said Marigold. "Like a whisper hour. We could ask Ms. Starr."

"Thanks." Sebastian looked from face to face. "I'm sorry I upset Marigold in the bathroom," he said.

"It's okay," Marigold said.

"Still. There wasn't any benefit to reading the graffiti. It just hurt your feelings."

She nodded.

"And I'm sorry I ruined hide-and-seek when we were at Sage. I didn't think about everyone else's fun. I just wanted to win."

"That wasn't so terrible," Bax said. "Honestly, I thought that was kind of awesome."

Sebastian laughed softly at that. Then all of them laughed together, softly, and the sound waves were pretty and gentle and just the right amount of bright.

18

Ms. Starr came over to the UDM kids with a tray of giant jelly beans (they were the size of mangoes!) and foot-long churros. Big treats for Big Night. Nory took a churro and a ginormous strawberry jelly bean.

Everyone's mouths were still full when Coach came over. He was drinking a green juice from a large mason jar. "Is my winning team ready for a visit to the top secret location?" he asked.

Of course they were!

Nory, Elliott, and Pepper followed Coach into

the hall on foot. Andres, who'd slipped free of his brickpack, accompanied them overhead. Coach led them upstairs to the library.

"Don't tell a soul where it is," he said when they got there. "Only the winners of the Big Night Scavenger Hunt have access to this room. It's a tradition that goes back more than twenty years." He handed each of them a key, strung on a bright green lanyard.

"But where is it?" asked Elliott. "I don't see a door or anything."

Coach put a finger to his lips. Tiptoeing, even though he didn't have to, he led the kids to a bookshelf against one wall, just an ordinary bookshelf like any other. "You have to press on this green book. Green like your lanyards, see?" said Coach. "It's titled *Secrets of the Book Room*."

Coach pressed the green book, and its spine popped open to reveal a lock. Nory and the others gasped.

"Nory, do you want to do the honors?" he asked.

Nory fitted her key into the lock and turned it. She

gave the bookshelf a push, and it opened inward to reveal a small room with a round window at one end.

It was beautiful. A thick carpet lay on the floor. Strings of paper snowflakes were laced across the ceiling. Bookshelves lined the walls—worn old paperbacks that had clearly been loved by lots of kids who had used the room before. There was a table with chairs by the window, and on the shelf nearest it were piles of games: Dragon Megamix, Catch the Unicorn, and stuff like that.

A bunch of beanbag chairs made a circle on one side, to make for comfy reading. One shelf held stacks of paper and two boxes of watercolor paint. There was a small sink in the corner and a mini fridge next to it.

"The key holders have access to this room until the next Big Night," said Coach. "Mr. Wang, the librarian, knows all about it. You can come in and use the room as early as an hour before school begins."

"We can have top secret breakfast meetings!" Nory exclaimed.

Coach nodded. "Or you can visit during recess. You can also use it till six in the evening."

"We'll never have to hide in the supply closet again," said Pepper.

"We can play games after school," said Andres.

"It's perfect," breathed Elliott.

It was. Sure, Nory wished she had four more keys so she could share the room with her other UDM friends, but she was sure she could invite them in.

More to the point: She had done it. She had won the scavenger hunt, and they had had the best Big Night ever. She and her team. She and Elliott.

"You'll stay now, right?" she said to him. "You can't leave this awesomeness."

Elliott looked confused. "What?"

"You can't leave us and go to Sage, now that we have this room," said Nory. "Nobody would give this up. Nobody."

"Nory," he answered, shaking his head. "I'm going to Sage, no matter what."

"But you just said the room was perfect."

"It is. But it'll be for you, Pepper, and Andres. I already made my decision."

Nory's eyes filled with tears. "But I thought . . ."

"I'm going," he told her gently. "It's the right choice for me, and my parents agree."

Pepper touched Nory's arm. "Having the secret room will still be great, Nory," she said. "We'll do our homework in here on the days you don't have kittenball club after school. We can keep candy in the cupboard. Ooh, and cold drinks in the fridge!"

"We can bring our Dreggs," said Andres.

Nory sighed. Those things did sound wonderful. But they would be so much more wonderful with Elliott.

He wouldn't ever be at Dunwiddle again, after tonight.

"I'll miss you loads," said Elliott, looking a little uncomfortable.

Nory walked slowly over to a beanbag chair. She nudged it with her toe. Then she sat down with a *woomph* and let the beanbag engulf her.

At the beginning of the night, everything had seemed so full of promise.

But now, *poof.* Her hopes of having Elliott stay at Dunwiddle forever had been dashed.

She knew, deep in her mind, that none of her friends would stay at Dunwiddle *forever.* Not even her. Because, you know, life.

Things changed.

People moved on.

The UDM kids would graduate from Dunwiddle and go to high school. Then maybe college. After that, who knew?

Also—her Big Night resolution. Elliott wasn't staying at Dunwiddle, so that resolution was pointless. What now?

Aunt Margo said a resolution was like a wish, but a wish you could make come true yourself.

What if . . . ?

Nory's throat felt tight. What if her resolution was to let go of her fantasy that Elliott would stay?

Could she just be happy and stay friends with him and figure out her life at Dunwiddle without him?

She hated the thought of Elliott not being here at Dunwiddle. But since it was his life, Nory supposed that maybe, just possibly, Elliott should get to decide how to live it.

Back in the gym, everything was all hustle and bustle. People were eating churros and goofing off, rummaging through their bags and talking. Andres put his brickpack back on, and the team returned to the UDM area. Willa and Marigold were sitting on Marigold's giant sleeping bag, making each other laugh. Bax was reading a book. Sebastian was sitting with his eyes closed, wearing his head cone and his goggles.

Nory approached Bax. "Is Sebastian okay?"

Bax looked up. "Not really. He's having a harder time then we realized. Much harder."

"Oh, no."

"Yeah. We're loud," Bax said. "Pretty much all the time. We yell, we bang doors, we're noisy. And it turns out that Sebastian's magic has been getting stronger. He can't control it, so his eyes and head always hurt."

Oh, wow, thought Nory. *Poor Sebastian.*

"We decided we're all going to be a lot quieter around him," Bax continued. "And we're not going to give him a hard time about his goggles or his head cone, ever."

Nory felt awful that Sebastian was in pain. "Right. Of course," she said.

Bax nodded and went back to his book.

Nory headed back toward Elliott, Pepper, and Andres, but she paused before she reached them.

She thought about Sebastian. She thought about life and magic and all the different ways people handled all sorts of different challenges.

She had an idea. "Elliott, what are you planning to do with your key to the secret room?"

"Give it to Lacey," he said with a straight face. "I feel like she deserves it."

"What?" Nory gasped.

"Kidding." Elliott grinned. "I don't know. Give it to someone in UDM, I guess. Who should have it?"

"Sebastian," Nory said. "Only, I'm actually thinking that we should *all* give him our keys."

"How come?" Andres asked.

"He's having a rotten time," explained Nory. She told them everything Bax had shared. They looked as sad as she had been. "See, if we give him the keys to the secret room," she ended, "then he'd have a special place, just for him. A quiet place. What do you think?"

"Great idea," Elliott said promptly.

Andres nodded slowly. "I'm in," he said. "I don't need the prize if it would help Sebastian."

"Me either," said Pepper. "And anyway, you and I have our supply-closet hideout."

They all four took off their lanyards.

19

After hearing about his headache, Ms. Starr had gently suggested that Sebastian could call his dads and go home. But Sebastian wanted to stay. He wanted to be with his friends. He wanted to fold his paper owl and release it into the night.

Also, Bax had asked if he wanted to hear the story of the ghost with no head later, when they were all in their sleeping bags. And Sebastian did. He could listen with his eyes closed.

He was doing more of his breathing exercises

when he felt a tap on his shoulder. He opened his eyes. "Yes?"

"Guess what!" Nory yelled. Then she lowered her voice. "Sorry. Quiet voice. Yes. Okay. We have a surprise for you! Our team does." She was standing with Pepper, Elliott, and Andres.

Nory pulled her hand from behind her back. In it were four green lanyards, each with a shiny key attached. "Your new special place," she said. "We're giving the secret room to you so you can have a quiet hideout."

What? Really? Sebastian didn't know what to say.

"I'll have to show you where it is, of course," Nory added.

"It's so cool in there," said Elliott. "It's got books and games and beanbag chairs."

"Plus a fridge," said Pepper.

Sebastian's eyes teared up behind his goggles. "Thank you," he said.

Nory beamed as she handed him the lanyards. "Any time."

Sebastian looked at his friends through the fog of his tears. Funny—the tears were blurring the sounds of the gym, making the bright sound waves a little less painful than they had been.

He looked at the lanyards, admiring their official appearance, and hung all four of them around his neck.

Ms. Starr brought the Upside-Down Magic class up to the roof to make their resolutions. Stars twinkled above. Snowflakes landed and melted on their clothes.

Everyone stood in a circle and held one of the paper owls they'd made in the cafeteria. "It's so pretty out here," Sebastian breathed. He loved the tiny flakes in the swirling wind. And the silence. The silence! No one was talking. The grandeur of the night had quieted them all.

Tentatively, he took off his head cone. Then his goggles. With his peripheral vision clear, he could see Bax on his left and Marigold on his right. He rubbed his temples where the goggles pressed and rolled his neck around.

"Kids, let's remember the Big Night owls and what they stand for," said Ms. Starr.

"Looking toward the future," Nory piped up, keeping her voice soft.

"Yes," said Ms. Starr. "Just as night always turns into day, there will always be endings that turn into new beginnings. So let's look toward the future and get ready to make our resolutions."

Sebastian had already decided on his resolution. He resolved to think before he spoke, and to try to see the world through other people's eyes. If he expected his friends to consider how he felt, he needed to make sure he did the same for them.

Ms. Starr beamed. "Listen for those invisible wings, 'kay?"

Hoot!

They all froze.

Hoot! Hoot!

"What was that?" Willa asked.

A large, dark gray owl swooped over them, circling above their group, flying in and out of the shadows of the night, showing itself briefly in the light from the open stairwell door.

"I think I hear wings," cried Nory. "Is it a Big Night owl?"

"Um, it's just a regular owl," said Sebastian. "But it doesn't seem the slightest bit scared. Pepper, is your magic paused?"

"Huh?" Pepper said. "My magic isn't paused. Where's the owl?" She looked around.

The owl settled on the ledge at the edge of the roof, tucking its wings around it, nearly disappearing into the night. But it was still clearly there, its round eyes wide.

"I want to see the owl," said Nory. "Where is it?"

Sebastian pointed right at it.

They all looked—right at it. Then at one another, their expressions confused. Then at Sebastian.

"You know," said Marigold. "You see the invisible world."

"And?" he asked.

"It's an invisible owl," she said. "A Big Night owl."

But Big Night owls didn't exist. They were like ghosts. The stuff of legends.

"I think Marigold is right," said Ms. Starr, her voice filled with awe. "You can see Big Night owls."

Zamboozle, thought Sebastian. *They do exist. They do!*

The Big Night owl spread its wings and took off, swooping around their group one more time before flying off into the night.

Goodbye, owl! thought Sebastian.

Seeing it reminded him how lucky he was. It was true, his magic was difficult and painful. But it also let him see a world that was beautiful and special and always changing.

20

"Is everyone ready?" Ms. Starr asked.

"Yes!" Nory chorused with the rest of her classmates.

The teacher smiled and lifted her own paper owl. "Ready. Set. Let those resolutions fly!"

They tossed their paper owls into the night air. As Nory tossed hers, she resolved to let go of Elliott and be happy for him. She would wish him well at Sage Academy, because that was what he wanted. And she'd find fun ways for them to stay friends while he was on his boarding school journey.

The little paper owls went every which way in the swirling snowstorm. Willa's owl face-planted itself by her feet, but she tried again and it took flight. Most of the others floated gently down from the rooftop toward the earth. But the owl belonging to Sebastian rose into the sky, whirling in the circling wind. Nory's owl went in the opposite direction, but also up and up and up.

After a moment, Ms. Starr cleared her throat. "Great job, kids. May all our resolutions lead to new and wonderful beginnings. And speaking of new beginnings . . . I have some exciting news to share." She pressed the tips of her fingers together. "After the winter break, a new student will be joining our class."

There was a murmur of voices.

"A new kid? Really?"

"An upside-down kid?"

"Of course, an upside-down kid."

"Halfway through the school year?"

"He won't know how to hula-hoop."

"Who says it's a boy?"

"Who says he—*or* she, or they—won't know how to hula-hoop?"

"What kind of magic does the new kid have? That's the thing that matters."

"Kids." Ms. Starr smiled. "The new student *is* a boy, and we'll be learning about his magic when he arrives at Dunwiddle. I just wanted you to know he was coming. That way, we can be a very welcoming group when we come back to school in January. Remember how you all felt on your first day in UDM? It's challenging, learning everyone's magics, getting used to studying in an alternative way. I'd like you all to put some real thought into how we can best welcome a new friend."

Nory wasn't sure how she felt. A new student. *Maybe* a new friend.

"We'll need to warn him about the Sparkies," said Andres.

"And the pizza bagels," said Sebastian.

"We should warn him about *us*," said Bax. "He

might not be ready for all the squippies and swivel chairs and stuff."

"He'll love those," said Willa. "They're super cool. But does he know to bring extra clothes? For when I rain?"

"He'll get to meet Carrot," said Pepper. "Carrot will make him happy be to be in UDM, right from the start."

Elliott's posture had stiffened, Nory could feel his tension.

"The new kid, whoever he is, won't replace you," Nory whispered.

"I know," said Elliott. He didn't meet her eyes.

"Okay, good," said Nory. "'Cause, like, you're not actually replaceable."

He smiled, and his shoulders visibly relaxed. "Don't go all mushy, Nory."

She smiled back at him. She would be mushy if she felt like it. She was with her UDM friends and her beloved teacher. They'd all be staying up late. There was going to be hot cocoa and maybe pizza and more gigantic jelly beans. And Big Night owls were definitely real.

Nory thought about what Ms. Starr had said: *Just as night always turns into day, there will always be endings that turn into new beginnings.* That was just life. There were lots of changes headed her way, and she couldn't control any of them.

But she could control how she handled them.

So, she would make the best of them.

Nory gazed at the sky. It was the longest night of the year. She was getting older. And maybe, possibly, wiser?

The snowflakes, the stars. The invisible Big Night owl.

Out there somewhere.

Acknowledgments

We'd like to send loads of giant strawberry jelly beans to the team at Scholastic, including but not limited to: David Levithan, Rachel Feld, Maya Marlette, Melissa Schirmer, Erin Berger, Taylan Salvati, Lauren Donovan, Lisa Bourne, Sue Flynn, Robin Hoffman, Lizette Serrano, Kelli Boyer, Emily Heddleson, Abby Dening, Juliana Kolesova, Elizabeth Parisi, and Aimee Friedman.

Our amazing agents and support team, we send you moon cookies and all our appreciation: Laura Dail, Barry Goldblatt, Tricia Ready, Elizabeth

Kaplan, Lauren Walters, Heather Weston, and Deb Shapiro. Also, we love Bob.

We send foot-long churros of gratitude to our families: Randy, Al, Jamie, Maya, Mirabelle, Alisha, Daniel, Ivy, Hazel, Todd, Chloe, and Anabelle. The cats, however—Lauren's and Emily's—were very little help; we hope they will step up their feline support for our future projects.

The *Upside-Down Magic* movie came out while we were writing this book, and it has been a tremendous thrill to see our characters on-screen, with added Disney magic. Thanks to Lauren Kisilevsky, Charles Pugliese, Nick Pustay, Josh Cagan, Suzanne Farwell, Susan Cartsonis, Joe Nussbaum, and the wonderful cast, crew, and designers.

We would also like to thank Robert Swanson, who invented air horns.

Finally, much love to our readers. We wish you a wonderful Big Night and hope you see the owls. The magic is all around you.

About the Authors

SARAH MLYNOWSKI is the author of many books for tweens, teens, and adults, including the *New York Times* bestselling Whatever After series, the Magic in Manhattan series, and *Gimme a Call*. She is also the co-creator of the traveling middle-grade book festival OMG Bookfest. She would like to be a Flicker so she could make the mess in her room invisible. Find her everywhere at @sarahmlynowski.

LAUREN MYRACLE is the *New York Times* best-selling author of many books for young readers, including the Winnie Years series, the Flower Power series, and the Life of Ty series. *The Backward Season* is the most recent book in her Wishing Day trilogy. Her co-authored book, *Let It Snow*, is a movie on Netflix. She would like to be a Fuzzy so she could talk to unicorns and feed them berries. You can find Lauren online at laurenmyracle.com.

EMILY JENKINS is the author of many chapter books, including *Harry Versus the First One Hundred Days of School*; *Brave Red, Smart Frog*; the Toys Trilogy (which begins with *Toys Go Out*) and the Invisible Inkling series. Her picture books include *All-of-a-Kind Family Hanukkah*; *A Greyhound, A Groundhog*; *Lemonade in Winter*; and *Toys Meet Snow*. She would like to be a Flare and work as a pastry chef. Visit Emily at emilyjenkins.com.